Angels Among Us

Sherief A. Abouelmagd

DEDICATION

To my friends and family—your unwavering love, encouragement, and presence have been the light guiding me through every chapter of this novel. You are the real angels among us, and this story is as much yours as it is mine.

CONTENTS

Chapter 1 - The Dream

She jumped out of bed in fear, looking around and, for a moment, disoriented, not knowing where she was. She heard a sound in her sleep calling her to wake up, but was this a dream? She looked around the bedroom and saw shadows on the walls, a reflection from street lights coming through the window. The alarm clock on the vanity shows the time 04:00 AM. She wondered, "What is happening?" The occurrence is not the first time, and it sounds real.

She got a hold of herself and lay back on her bed, staring at the ceiling, and said, "I am stressed; it's just a dream." After a short while, she fell back into sleep again. The alarm went off at 07:00; she jumped out of bed and into the shower to get ready for another busy day at the office.

Emilia is a 35-year-old businesswoman who owns a beautiful townhouse in Fairfax, Virginia, where she has lived for the past five years and works as a bank branch manager.

The two-story townhouses overlook a beautiful garden with

large trees. This is the season when cherry blossom trees coincide with the arrival of spring. The pink flowers are breathtaking, and it's a wonderful view to start your day.

Emilia, dressed in her business attire, walks out to the back deck on the ground floor holding her cup of coffee, running her fingers through her long dangling blonde hair, and looking at the beautiful scene of the garden with flowers dancing with the morning breeze. She sat down on the chair and just remembered what happened in her dream.

A few minutes later, she jumps into her red convertible Mercedes and drives to work, a fifteen-minute drive, while she enjoys listening to soothing morning music and browsing through her mobile phone during traffic light stops to check her busy schedule. Today she has an important appointment with an investor who is planning to open a multimillion-dollar shopping mall in the city. The closing of such a large loan for the bank is crucial, and with Emilia's charm, finesse, and experience, she is able to bring it home.

Her large office is located on the 2nd floor of the bank at the end of the hall next to a large, well-equipped boardroom. As she walks by, she sees her branch assistant Jennifer laying down folders on the large table, preparing for the meeting. In addition to being her assistant, Jennifer has been a close friend since high school. They went to the same college and enjoyed their teenage years together. She could not picture her life without her being part of it. Jennifer is one year younger and attractive with dark skin, a slim body, and black curly hair. She has always been the one with a sense of humor and a unique approach, whereas Emilia tends to resist and rely more on logic.

Emilia popped her head into the boardroom without Jennifer noticing, and she looked at her with admiration and a large smile on her face. She has been thinking all morning about sharing the dream with her. Nevertheless, she was determined to open the subject today, as she can't keep the memory to herself anymore.

"Morning, Jenny," she said with a faded voice. Jennifer turned around and jumped with joy at seeing her, but she instantly knew something was wrong. She walked towards her and grabbed her arm to sit her down on one of the chairs and asked what is going on. Emilia hesitated for a moment but then started to tell the story. She explained that for the past three days, a strange dream has woken her up every night at 4 am. She is confused, frightened, and doesn't know why this is happening. Jenny, being her usual self, dismissed what she had heard and attributed the nightmares to stress. Emilia has a lot going on in her personal and work life, which keeps her mind occupied and causes her to overthink, potentially disrupting her sleep. She has some life-changing decisions to make, which could be the reason.

"Same dream, same time, for three days!" Emilia exclaimed as she stared at her, locked eyes with her, and proclaimed. She hears what seems like a young woman calling her to open her eyes. Putting her hand on her shoulder, Jenny sat down in the chair beside her and urged her to relax. All of these phenomena must have an explanation, she said. Having recurring dreams is strange, but it could be a subconscious warning that you're about to make a life-altering decision.

Emilia was brought up by loving and caring parents who taught her well. She is not only beautiful and smart but also well-mannered and has strong beliefs that good things happen for good people, which is how she portrays herself to the world around her. A year ago, she met her soulmate, "Sam," who became the love of her life. She was fortunate to meet such a passionate man who filled her world with happiness.

Since they met, they were never apart until disaster struck two weeks earlier. Sam, in his early 40s, tall and smart-looking, has been working at a large financial firm for the past ten years and has built a successful career managing large funds. He owns a house in the same compound where Emilia lives, and they met coincidentally at the clubhouse a year earlier in one of the community events. It was love at first sight, and both realized they wanted to be together forever.

Two weeks earlier, Sam invited Emilia to a dinner at a luxury and expensive Japanese restaurant where they planned to enjoy their favorite sushi and cocktails. They agreed to meet at 8pm at the venue. Emilia made sure to wear her nice, tight red dress for the occasion. The ambiance was just perfect; the romantic music filled the air with warmth, and it was the right moment. Sam had planned the moment for a while and was nervous but excited to make this big decision. He sipped on his cocktails one after another while Emilia looked at him with love and admiration.

Finally, Sam stood up from his chair and knelt on the floor next to her. She was smart and immediately knew what was going on. In fact, she has waited for this moment, and here it is. He proposed to marry her, holding out a diamond ring. The moment was breathtaking; she stood up and hugged him really hard, telling him how much she loves him. Sam had briefed the restaurant manager earlier, and when he opened the champagne, all the guests clapped and cheered.

The night was just young, and they made sure to enjoy every moment. The drinks kept pouring in until they had enough. It was almost midnight, and they walked out of the restaurant, handing their valet tickets to the attendant to bring their cars. Emilia jumped in her Mercedes and told him she would be waiting for him at home to continue their celebration and took off. Sam was not feeling well and could hardly get into his car. The attendant proposed to call a cab for him, but he declined, jumped in his car, and went on his way.

Sam was super excited from the night events; he could not have been happier. He cranked up the music and accelerated, surpassing the speed limit. The streets were empty, and hardly any cars were passing by. He was looking at his phone regularly while driving to view the pictures taken during the night, admiring the beauty of Emilia, and dreaming of what would come next. In fact, what came next was a disaster. His left hand held the steering wheel and his right reached under the chair to retrieve the phone, which he dropped on the floor.

He could not reach the phone and had to look down for a second to see where it is. In that moment—the life-changing moment of his life— he missed seeing a red traffic light ahead and continued at the same speed. He grabbed the phone and started to look up, and this is when it happened.

He saw the mercury grey van a few inches in front of his car crossing the intersection, and in a split second, before even having a chance to react, he smashed into the back left side of the van, which turned in circles and fell on its side. Sam slammed hard on the brakes, and his car stopped about 50 meters into the street ahead. His airbag opened in time and saved him from hitting the steering wheel; he looked up in the mirror in disbelief and saw the van in the corner of the intersection.

Sam was in shock and could not believe what just happened. His intoxication prevented him from thinking clearly. He reached for the door to open it but hesitated. He looked again in the back mirror; the van was still on its side, no one in the street, no movement. He did not know what to do; he was so scared. He wondered whether it was his mistake or not since he did not see the red traffic light. But the panic got hold of him, and he could not control his thinking or emotions. Finally, he decided to press the accelerator and drive away, erasing everything that had transpired. He reached his house and parked his car in the garage. He looked around to make sure no one was watching.

Stepping into his living room, he was trembling and disoriented, then sat down on the living sofa and turned on his TV to the local news to see if the accident was reported. He looked into the mirror to check his face, which did not have any scratches. He was lucky; the airbag and seatbelt saved his life.

Emilia had no idea what had transpired that night. She waited for Sam at home, her heart still fluttering with excitement from the proposal. As the minutes turned into hours, worry began to creep in. She tried calling Sam's phone, but there was no answer. She reasoned that maybe he had run into some old friends or had stopped somewhere to celebrate a little longer. Emilia eventually fell asleep on the couch, still in her red dress, clutching her phone.

The next morning, she awoke with a start, immediately checking her phone. She checked her phone but found no messages or missed calls. Panic set in as she tried calling him again, but there was still no response. She hurriedly got dressed and decided to drive over to his house. As she pulled into his driveway, she saw his car parked in the garage. Relief washed over her; he was home.

Sam opened the door, his face pale and eyes bloodshot. Before Emilia could say anything, he pulled her inside and closed the door. He began to recount the events of the previous night, his voice trembling. Emilia listened in shock as he confessed to the accident. The weight of his actions hung heavily in the air. She held his hands tightly, trying to calm him down, but her mind was racing. They needed to figure out what to do next. The love and happiness of the previous night seemed like a distant memory, overshadowed by the grim reality of the present.

Sam paced the living room, his eyes darting toward the clock every few seconds. Emilia sat on the couch, her hands clasped tightly together, trying to process everything he had told her. When she inquired why he did not stop and go back to check on the people in the van, Sam replied he was in shock; he was afraid of what to see; he was confused. The decision he made currently was wrong, but that is what it is. The shock and fear in Sam's eyes were palpable, and she knew the gravity of the situation. They had no information whatsoever to go by and didn't know what happened to the people in the van or who they are. Sam's only knowledge is that the vehicle appeared to be a grey Mercury van, with no further details available.

It had been two days since the accident, and there had been no news, no sign of the disaster Sam had left behind. Emilia couldn't shake the feeling of dread that hung over them. Every time she closed her eyes; she pictured the accident and Sam's terrified expression. They needed to find out what had happened to the people in the van.

For the next few days, they scoured TV news reports, scanned newspapers, and checked online news outlets, but there was no mention of the accident. The silence was both a relief and a source of anxiety. What if the authorities were still investigating? What if they came knocking at Sam's door?

Then, one evening, as Emilia was flipping through the channels with Sam nearby, a breaking news report caught her attention. The anchor's solemn tone shivered through her. A hit-and-run accident that occurred a week ago was now under investigation. Another vehicle struck the victims, a family of three, as they were driving home. The driver, Adam, suffered minor injuries, but his pregnant wife, Stephanie, was in critical condition at the county hospital. Their unborn child was also in danger. Police were appealing for any witnesses or information about the vehicle involved. The reporter further explained that the cameras available surveyed by the police could only see the side of the van after being hit and a quick glimpse of the runaway SUV, which caused the accident but gave them no more leads, so basically, they cannot identify the van or the owner. The police were pleading for anyone who has information to come forward.

Emilia's heart sank. She turned to Sam, who was staring at the screen, his face ashen. It was them—the family from the accident. Sam's knees gave way, and he collapsed onto the couch, overwhelmed by guilt and fear.

The full extent of the consequences hit them. Sam was paralyzed with fear, the weight of his actions pressing down on him like a physical force. He couldn't bring himself to go to the police; the thought of ruining his career and facing the legal consequences was too much to bear. Emilia, torn between her love for Sam and her conscience, felt a growing sense of dread. She had always believed in doing the right thing, but this situation was testing her principles.

The atmosphere was tense. Sam was pacing again while Emilia sat at the dining table, her mind in turmoil. The news about Stephanie and the baby had hit her hard, and she couldn't shake the feeling of responsibility. They couldn't keep this a secret, she thought. Those people were suffering because of them, but Sam insisted he did not want to go forward. He thought the pain would pass; he thought the mother and baby would be fine.

As the days passed, Emilia's inner conflict grew. She had mixed emotions. She knows what happened, but Sam does not want to report it or take action. She searched daily for news but with no luck. No Clue what happened to the Stephanie and the baby. She goes to bed every day thinking of them.

She found herself waking up at 4 a.m., the same haunting dream replaying in her mind. The young woman's voice pleading with her to open her eyes echoed in her ears. She knew it was her conscience trying to tell her something. The guilt was unbearable, and she knew they had to do the right thing, even if it meant risking everything.

Back in the office, Jennifer turned to Emilia and told her to take a deep breath. She has an important client meeting to close an important contract for the bank, and she needs to concentrate. She assured her she will be beside her every step of the way to figure out what is going on. Jenny's words soothed her, and she proceeded with her routine as usual. Later she went home after work, exhausted. She has not seen Sam for the past couple of days. She felt staying away from him for a few days would be a beneficial thing so she could think and gather her thoughts. She had a light dinner and went to bed early.

Chapter 2 - The Angel

The familiar sound of the young woman's voice echoed in her ears as she woke up, pleading with her to open her eyes. Her heart pounded in her chest as she glanced around the room. This time, something was different. The shadows on the walls seemed to dance with an ethereal light, and she felt a presence in the room. She glanced at the alarm clock on the vanity—4:00 AM, again.

A shiver ran down her spine as she noticed a figure standing at the foot of her bed. It was a woman, but not just any woman—this figure looked like a more radiant, ethereal version of herself. Emilia's breath caught in her throat as the figure spoke in a calm, soothing voice.

"Please, calm down. Don't be afraid. I will explain everything."

Emilia's first instinct was to reach for the bedside lamp. She turned it on, flooding the room with a warm, yellow light. She blinked, expecting the figure to disappear.

But to her astonishment, the angelic version of herself was still there, glowing with a soft, otherworldly light.

"Who... what are you?" Emilia stammered, her voice trembling with fear and confusion.

"I am your guardian angel," the figure replied gently. "I am here to guide you, to help you find your way through this difficult time. Please, remain calm and listen to what I have to say."

Emilia's mind raced. Such an experience couldn't be real and had to be a dream. But everything felt so vivid— so tangible. She could feel the soft fabric of her nightgown against her skin, the coolness of the room, and the warmth of the light from the lamp. And the angel's voice was so soothing, so real.

As the angel began to speak, Emilia felt a sense of peace wash over her, despite the fear and confusion lingering in her mind. The angel told her that her recurring dreams were not just figments of her imagination. They were messages, warnings about the path she and Sam were on.

"You and Sam are bound by love, but you are also bound by the choices you have made," the angel said. "The accident was a turning point, a moment where the course of your lives changed dramatically. You must face the consequences of that night, but you must also find a way to heal, to seek forgiveness and redemption."

Emilia's eyes filled with tears as she listened. The weight of the past two weeks, the guilt, the fear, the uncertainty—it all came crashing down on her. She had tried to bury it, to push it aside, but now, hearing these words, she knew she couldn't ignore it any longer.

"What should I do?" Emilia whispered, her voice choked with emotion. She asked the angel how she can make things right.

The angel's expression softened, and she reached out, placing a hand on Emilia's shoulder. The touch was warm and comforting.

"Follow your heart, Emilia. Do what you know is right. You have the strength within you to face this— to make amends. Trust in yourself, and trust in those who love you. You are not alone."

As Emilia blinked through her tears, the angel's form began to shimmer and fade. "Remember, I am always with you, even if you cannot see me. Have faith, and all will be well."

Before she could respond, the angel vanished, leaving Emilia alone in the dimly lit room. She sat there for a moment, trying to process what had just happened. Had it been real? Was it truly her guardian angel, or just another dream?

She knew she needed to talk to someone. She grabbed her phone and dialed Jennifer's number. It was early, but Jennifer answered almost immediately, her voice groggy with sleep.

Jenny could sense the urgency in Emilia's voice, and she was sure something had happened. Emilia tried to explain but could not; she was not making any sense. Jenny instructed her to end the call, grab a cup of tea, and quickly make her way to her townhouse.

As Emilia waited for Jennifer, she tried to collect her thoughts.

The angel's words echoed in her mind, bringing a strange sense of calm amidst the turmoil. She knew that facing the truth was the only way forward, no matter how frightening it seemed.

Jennifer arrived, still in her pajamas, and rushed inside. Emilia wasted no time, pouring out everything that had happened, the recurring dreams, the angelic visitation, and the overwhelming guilt about the accident. Jennifer listened intently, her eyes wide with a mixture of disbelief and concern. When Emilia finished, Jennifer took a deep breath.

"Em, I think you're under a lot of stress. What you're going through with Sam, it's enough to make anyone's mind play tricks," she paused, and her expression softened. "But I believe you."

Emilia nodded, feeling a renewed sense of determination. "The angel said I need to do what's right. I think that means we need to go to the police and tell them everything. Sam and I can't keep running from this."

Jennifer squeezed Emilia's hand. "I'll be with you every step of the way. We'll get through this together."

Due to the night events and lack of sleep, Emilia elected to take the day off and remain at home. Her mind was in disbelief of what happened, and her encounter with the angel gave her a strange but soothing feeling that things will be alright. At night, she fell asleep with a sense of resolve. As she drifted into slumber, she hoped for the angel to return, to guide her once more. And sure enough, the angel appeared in her dream, the same as the night before, calling for her to wake up.

Emilia woke up this time, the angel's words still echoing in her mind. As before, the angel stood at the foot of her bed as she looked around. This time, she did not turn on the light. Instead, she took a deep breath, trying to calm her racing heart.

The angel smiled. "You are ready, Emilia. You have the strength to face what lies ahead. Trust in yourself." With those words, Emilia stepped out of bed and walked towards her angel, this time with no fear, then sat next to her on the chair. She asked the angel to explain more about what was going on, why she was here, how she could see her, etc. Emilia had a plethora of questions, and her angel instructed her to grab a cup of coffee, after which she would provide a detailed explanation.

Emilia, coffee in hand, settled back into her chair, her eyes locked on the angel who sat across from her, radiating a soft, warm glow. She felt a sense of anticipation mingled with curiosity, ready to understand the deeper reasons behind the angel's presence.

The angel began to speak, her voice a soothing melody in the quiet room. "Emilia, guardian angels like myself appear to certain people at pivotal moments in their lives. These moments often involve significant choices, challenges, or changes. We come to provide guidance, support, and clarity when it is most needed."

Emilia leaned forward, hanging on to every word. "But why me? Why now? And why can only I see you?"

The angel's eyes softened with understanding. "You are at a crossroads, Emilia. The events with Sam and the accident have created a ripple in your life that affects not only your future but the lives of others. Your heart and mind are in turmoil, and your soul has called out for guidance. That is why I am here—to help you navigate these turbulent waters and find the right path."

Emilia nodded slowly, absorbing the angel's words. "But why can't anyone else see you? Why is it just me?"

The angel smiled gently. "Our presence is revealed only to those who are ready and willing to accept our guidance. It is a deeply personal and spiritual connection. Your openness and desire for understanding have allowed you to see me. Others, like Jennifer, can sense something is different, but they cannot see me unless they, too, reach a point of readiness in their lives."

Emilia took a sip of her coffee, the warmth grounding her as she processed this information. "So, you're saying that this is about my readiness to face the truth and make the right decisions?"

"Exactly," the angel replied. "You have been given this opportunity to seek redemption, to heal, and to bring light into a dark situation. Your recurring dreams were your soul's way of alerting you to the importance of these choices. Now, with my guidance, you can move forward with confidence and clarity."

Emilia, feeling a mix of anticipation and apprehension, continued to listen intently to the angel's soothing voice.

"There is more you need to know, Emilia," the angel said, her expression growing more serious. "Now that I've shown up, be ready for the next arrival." This presence will not be like mine;

it will be the Trouble angel, whose role is to challenge and confuse you."

Emilia's eyes widened. "Another angel? Trouble angel? What do you mean?"

The angel nodded gently. "Every person is followed by two angels: a guardian angel, like myself, who guides and protects, and a trouble angel who monitors and records the less favorable actions and decisions. This trouble angel will appear to you as well, but do not be afraid. While I resemble a better version of you, the trouble angel will appear as the worst version of yourself. They embody the fears, doubts, and negative traits that you try to overcome."

Emilia's heart skipped a beat at the thought of encountering a darker version of herself. "What will they do? Will they try to harm me?"

The angel shook her head, her expression calm and reassuring. "No, they cannot harm you, nor can they force you to do anything. Both of us are here to guide you through this challenging time, but in different ways. Angel Malika, that is her name, will try to confuse you, to make you doubt yourself and your decisions. It is their way of testing your resolve and pushing you to confront the darker aspects of your soul. Remember, they can only influence you through words, not actions."

Emilia took another sip of her coffee, trying to steady her nerves. "So, I need to listen to both of you and make my own decisions?"

"Precisely," the angel replied. "You are ultimately in control of your choices. Our presence is meant to guide you, to help you see different perspectives, and to understand the consequences of your actions. Once you resolve the situation and discover the right path, we will both vanish.

Emilia felt a strange sense of empowerment. "I think I understand. This isn't just about the accident with Sam; it's about facing my fears and making the right choices for my life." The angel smiled warmly. "Exactly, Emilia. Trust in yourself, have faith in your strength, and remember that you are never alone. You are supported by those who love you, and you have the inner strength to face whatever comes your way."

Emilia looked back and asked if the Angel has a name and she replied you can call me "Angel Mila". She further explained that the guardian angel name is always the host name and, in this case, "Angel Mila" and the trouble angel name would start with the same first letter of the host name, and in this case "Angel Malika".

With those words, the angel's form began to shimmer and fade once more, leaving Emilia alone in the quiet room. As the first light of dawn began to filter through the curtains, she felt a renewed sense of determination. She knew that the journey ahead would be difficult, but she also knew that she had the strength and guidance to face it. And with Jennifer by her side and the angels' presence in her life, she was ready to confront the challenges that lay ahead.

Chapter 3 - The Accident

At the hospital, Adam sat by Stephanie's bedside, holding her hand and whispering words of encouragement. The hospital room was filled with the steady beeping of monitors, and the sterile smell of antiseptics hung in the air. Stephanie's pale face was a stark contrast to her usual vibrant self, and Adam's heart ached to see her in this state.

Adam, a 30-year-old Native American from Miami, Florida, working as a civil engineer for a midsize company in Fairfax, had been married to Stephanie for a year and was eagerly anticipating the arrival of their first child. After accepting a job offer from a new company, he relocated to Virginia and rented an apartment in a small community near his office. Stephanie, who loved the marketing world, worked as a social media freelancer and has been supporting Adam with her average income.

The accident had shattered their world, and now Adam was

grappling with the uncertainty of their future. As he sat there, the events of that night—the sudden impact, the van spinning out of control, and the sickening sound of metal against metal— repeated in his mind. He felt a pang of guilt for not being able to protect Stephanie and their baby.

Adam sat in the dimly lit hospital room, the constant beeping of monitors a haunting reminder of Stephanie's fragile state. Her pale face, framed by the stark white sheets, seemed almost lifeless. He could see the rise and fall of her chest, but it was shallow and labored. His heart ached with each breath she took, knowing that their unborn child was also fighting for life inside her.

He tightened his grip on Stephanie's hand, whispering words of encouragement. "Stay with me, Stephanie. We need you. Our baby needs you." His voice trembled, and tears welled up in his eyes. He couldn't imagine a future without her, without their child. The accident had shattered their world, leaving them teetering on the edge of a precipice.

A soft knock on the door interrupted his thoughts. A police officer stepped into the room; his expression serious but compassionate. "Mr. Adam, I'm Officer Davis. I need to ask you a few questions about the accident."

Adam nodded; his voice was hoarse. "I will help, but it all happened so fast."

Officer Davis took out a notepad. "Do you remember anything about the car that hit you? Could you recall the car's color, make, or model? Did you see the driver?"

Adam squeezed his eyes shut, trying to recall the chaotic moments. "It was dark... maybe black or dark blue. I didn't see the driver. Everything happened so quickly."

The officer nodded, jotting down notes. "Thank you, Mr. Adam. We'll keep you updated on the investigation. I hope your wife and child recover soon."

As the officer left, Adam slumped back in his chair, feeling helpless. Hours passed in a blur as he sat by Stephanie's side, holding her hand and praying for a miracle. The doctors and nurses came and went, their faces grim, their voices hushed.

Just as Adam was about to drift into an exhausted sleep, the door to the room opened again. This time, it was a doctor he hadn't seen before. She was tall and composed, her dark hair pulled back into a neat bun. Her eyes were sharp but kind.

"Mr. Adam, I'm Dr. Isabella Martinez, the head surgeon. Can we speak outside for a moment?"

Adam's heart sank at her tone. He nodded and followed her into the hallway, his legs feeling like lead. Dr. Martinez led him to a quiet corner where they could talk privately.

"Mr. Adam," she began gently, "I'm afraid I have some difficult news. Your wife's condition has worsened, and so has the baby's. We're doing everything we can, but we're at a critical juncture."

Adam's breath caught in his throat. "What do you mean?"

Dr. Martinez took a deep breath, her expression somber. "We need to make a decision, and it's one that only you can make. We can attempt to save the baby, but it would mean an increased risk to Stephanie's life. Alternatively, we could concentrate on saving Stephanie, but this would not only result in the loss of the baby, but also put Stephanie's survival during the operation at high risk, potentially leading to the loss of both.

Adam felt the world spin around him. "No, there has to be another way. You can't ask me to choose between my wife and my child."

Dr. Martinez placed a hand on his shoulder. "I'm so sorry, Mr. Adam. We're doing everything we can, but we need to act quickly in the coming days."

Adam leaned against the wall, his mind racing. How could he reasonably be expected to make such a challenging decision? Every fiber of his being screamed in protest. He loved Stephanie more than anything, but the thought of losing their unborn child was unbearable.

After a long, agonizing silence, Adam nodded numbly. "I need to be with Stephanie. I need to talk to her."

Dr. Martinez nodded and led him back to Stephanie's room. Adam took her hand in his, his heart breaking. "Stephanie, please wake up. I need you to help me decide. I can't do this alone."

The minutes dragged on, and Adam felt more and more overwhelmed. Finally, he couldn't take it anymore. He kissed

28

Stephanie's forehead and whispered, "I love you," before leaving the room to get some air. He needed to clear his head so he could think.

He drove home in a daze, the weight of the decision pressing down on him. When he finally stumbled through the front door, he collapsed onto the couch, his mind and body exhausted. He closed his eyes, hoping for a moment of peace.

That was when he felt a presence in the room. He opened his eyes and saw a figure standing before him. It was a man, but not just any man—this figure looked like a more radiant, ethereal version of himself. The figure's calm, soothing voice caused Adam's breath to catch in his throat.

"Please, calm down. Don't be afraid. I will explain everything." Said "Angel Adam" Adam's Guardian Angel.

Chapter 4 - The Trouble angel

Emilia fell back into bed, her mind a whirlwind of thoughts and emotions. She finally drifted into a restless sleep, only to be awakened again by the same haunting sound. But this time, something was different. She glanced at the clock—4:00 AM, as always—and felt a presence in the room. She turned and saw a figure at the foot of her bed, but it wasn't the Emilia's Guardian Angel she had grown accustomed to.

This figure looked like a disheveled, slightly sinister version of herself, with wild hair, dark circles under her eyes, and a mischievous grin. Emilia sat up, her fear replaced by curiosity and a touch of annoyance.

"Great, another one," Emilia muttered, rubbing her eyes. "Who are you?"

The figure chuckled, a sound that was both eerie and oddly familiar. "I'm your Trouble angel, darling. Think of me as the sassier, funnier version of your guardian angel."

Emilia raised an eyebrow. "Trouble angel? Really?"

"Yup! Call me Angel Malika", plopping down on the edge of Emilia's bed. "I'm here to spice things up a bit. You're too serious with all this guilt and redemption stuff. Let's have some fun!"

Emilia couldn't help but laugh at the absurdity of it all. "Alright, Angel Malika. What kind of Trouble are you here to cause?"

Angel Malika leaned in, her grin widening. "I'm here to give you some advice. This advice contradicts the words of your guardian angel. It'll be hilarious!"

Emilia shook her head, amused and exasperated. "And why would I listen to you?"

Angel Malika shrugged. "Why not? You've got two angels now. Might as well hear both sides of the story."

Angel Malika's suggestions for solutions to Emilia's problems quickly turned their conversation into a comedic back-and-forth. Every time Angel Malika spoke, Emilia couldn't help but laugh, despite the seriousness of her situation.

"You should totally quit your job and become a professional juggler," Angel Malika suggested, her eyes twinkling with mischief.

Emilia snorted. "And how would that help with my current predicament?"

"It wouldn't," Angel Malika said with a wink. "But it would be fun!"

As they continued their banter, Emilia felt a strange sense of relief. Angel Malika's humor and lightheartedness were a welcome distraction from the heavy burden she had been carrying. But she also remembered the guardian angel's words, urging her to do what was right.

Just as Emilia was about to drift back to sleep, she felt another presence in the room. She opened her eyes to see both Angel Mila and Angel Malika standing before her, their contrasting auras creating a surreal scene.

"Alright, you two," Emilia said, sitting up and rubbing her temples. "What's the deal? Why are you both here?"

Angel Mila replied instantly, "We are here to guide you, Emilia. Each in our own way."

"And I'm here to make sure you don't get too boring," Angel Malika added with a wink.

The three of them spent the rest of the night in a lively, humorous conversation, with Angel Malika's antics and the guardian angel's calm wisdom providing a bizarre but entertaining dynamic. As the first light of dawn began to filter through the curtains, Emilia felt a strange sense of camaraderie with her two angelic companions.

"So, when do you guys disappear?" Emilia asked, stifling a yawn.

Angel Mila and Angel Malika exchanged a glance before replying in unison, "We don't."

Emilia's eyes widened. "You mean you're going to be with me 24/7?"

"Yup!" Angel Malika said, clapping her hands together. "We're your new best friends!"

Emilia was shocked but couldn't help but chuckle at the absurdity of it all. "Well, I guess I'd better get used to it."

With her two angels in tow, Emilia headed to work, feeling a strange mix of anxiety and amusement. The angels moved and acted like humans, but no one else could see them. They would occasionally pass through people, causing Emilia to stifle giggles.

In the office, Jennifer immediately noticed something was off. "Um, what's going on? You look... different."

Emilia took a deep breath and decided to come clean. "Jenny, I need to tell you something. I've been having these... visions. Of angels which I mentioned to you before. They're with me right now."

Jennifer's eyes widened. "Angels? Really?"

"Yes," Emilia replied. "And they're standing right here."

Jennifer looked around, clearly not seeing anything. Emilia decided to prove it.

"Jenny, go to your office, write a word on a piece of paper, and leave it on your desk. Come back here, and I'll tell you what it says," Emilia instructed.

Jennifer, looking skeptical but intrigued, did as she was told. When she returned, Emilia asked her guardian angel to go to Jennifer's office and read the word. The guardian angel complied and returned with the information.

"The word is 'hope,'" Emilia said confidently.

Jennifer's jaw dropped. "How did you know?" She started spinning around the room, trying to catch sight of the invisible angels. Angel Malika laughed, and Angel Mila smiled gently.

Jennifer, still trying to process everything, asked for another confirmation. Emilia obliged, and once again, Angel Mila delivered the correct word. Jennifer finally sat down, her disbelief turning into amusement.

"This is insane," Jennifer said, shaking her head. However, she found it somewhat intriguing. You've got your angel entourage!"

Emilia laughed. "Yeah, something like that."

Jennifer then dropped to her knees dramatically. "Emilia, you are the chosen one! Guide us mere mortals with your angelic wisdom!"

They both burst into laughter, and Emilia felt a weight lift off her shoulders. Jennifer's humor and acceptance made the situation less daunting.

"Seriously, though," Jennifer said, sitting back down. "You're lucky to have them. There's got to be a reason for all this. We'll figure it out together."

Jennifer invited Emilia and the angels to dinner at her house. Jennifer set places for the angels at the table, despite Emilia's explanation that they don't eat, drink, or see anyone but herself.

Over dinner, the four of them—Emilia, Jennifer, and the two angels—engaged in a deep and philosophical conversation about the relationship between humans and angels. Emilia continuously relays back to Jennifer what the angels say. They discussed the idea of coexisting without seeing each other and whether angels really have an impact on human lives.

"Have you ever wondered," Angel Mila began, "how often we interact with humans without them even realizing it?"

Jennifer leaned in, fascinated. "Tell us more. Do you have any stories?"

Angel Mila smiled gently. "There was a man named Thomas. He was at a crossroads in his life, unsure of which path to take. He felt lost, overwhelmed by the pressures of his job and personal life. One night, as he was walking home, he felt an inexplicable urge to take a different route. On this new path, he encountered an old friend he hadn't seen in years. That friend provided him with the advice and support he needed to make a crucial decision. Thomas believed it was a mere coincidence, but it was our gentle nudge that led him there."

Jennifer's eyes widened. "That's wonderful. So, you actually influence our decisions?"

"Not directly," Angel Mila clarified. "We offer guidance and gentle nudges. The choices are always yours to make."

Angel Malika leaned back, smirking. "I've got a story too. There was this woman named Rachel who was about to make a huge mistake—quitting her stable job to pursue something she wasn't prepared for. I gave her a little push to reconsider, and she ended up taking a course that made her realize her true passion. She didn't see it as divine intervention, just a change of heart."

Emilia laughed. "You mean you actually did something helpful?"

Angel Malika winked. "Hey, I'm not all Trouble angel. Occasionally a little chaos leads to clarity."

Jennifer shook her head in disbelief. "So, you're both here to guide us in your ways. It's incredible to think about how many times you might have influenced our lives without us knowing." Angel Mila nodded. "We are always here, whether you see us or not. Our purpose is to help you grow, learn, and navigate the complexities of life."

Emilia took a sip of her drink, pondering their words. "It's comforting to know you're here. But it also makes me wonder how many times I might have ignored your guidance." Angel

Mila's expression softened. "It's never too late to listen, Emilia. The important thing is that you're aware of our presence now."

Jennifer, ever the pragmatist, leaned forward with a mischievous glint in her eye. "So, if you two are always around, can you tell me what the winning lottery numbers are?"

Angel Mila and Angel Malika exchanged amused glances. "We're here to guide you on matters of the soul and heart, not to make you rich," Angel Mila replied gently. Angel Malika snickered. "But if I knew, I wouldn't tell you either. Where's the fun in that?"

They all laughed, the atmosphere lightening with each shared story and joke. As the night wore on, the conversation turned more philosophical.

"Do you think we, as humans, have the power to influence you angels?" Emilia asked, curiosity burning in her eyes.

Angel Mila nodded thoughtfully. "Absolutely. Your actions, thoughts, and emotions resonate with us. When you act with kindness and compassion, it strengthens our connection. When you are fearful or lost, it gives us more purpose to guide you back to your path."

Angel Malika added, "And when you make hilarious mistakes, it gives us something to laugh about. It's a symbiotic relationship."

Jennifer chuckled. "So, we're entertainment for you too?"

"Sometimes," Angel Malika said with a wink. "But mostly, we're here because we care. Your lives are meaningful, and our role is to help you see that."

The conversation flowed effortlessly, weaving through topics of fate, free will, and the unseen bonds between angels and humans. As the night deepened, a sense of peace settled over the table.

Jennifer looked at Emilia with a newfound respect. "You're lucky, you know. Not everyone gets to have such an encounter. There's a good reason for this. Emilia smiled, feeling the warmth of friendship and the guidance of her angels. "Thank you, Jenny. I couldn't do this without you."

Jennifer raised her glass. "To angels, seen and unseen, and to the adventures ahead." They clinked glasses, and the evening ended on a note of hope and camaraderie.

Later, at home, Emilia went to bed with the two angels by her side. She drifted off to sleep, knowing that whatever challenges lay ahead, she would face them with her guardian angel's wisdom and Angel Malika's humor by her side.

As the night went on, Emilia felt a sense of peace and acceptance. The angels' presence, though unusual, had become a source of comfort and guidance.

Meanwhile, back at Adam's place, he sat on the couch, his head in his hands, trying to process the weight of the decision he had to make. The stillness of the house was suddenly interrupted by a loud, mocking voice.

"Well, well, well, if it isn't Mr. Indecisive himself," the voice drawled. Adam looked up, startled, to see a figure standing in the doorway. It was a man, but not just any man—this figure looked like a disheveled, sarcastic version of himself, with a permanent smirk and an exaggerated swagger.

"Who are you?" Adam asked, his voice tinged with irritation and exhaustion.

The figure chuckled, a sound dripping with mockery. "Name's Angel Adil". Think of me as your less-than-helpful angelic guide. I'm here to make sure your life stays as complicated as possible."

Adam groaned inwardly. "Great, just what I needed. Another angel."

Angel Adil sauntered over, plopping down on the couch next to Adam and stretching out lazily. "Oh, come on, don't be like that. I'm here to spice things up. Perhaps you could consider flipping a coin to make the decision. Heads, save the wife. Tails, save the baby. Easy peasy."

Adam stared at him in disbelief. "You can't be serious."

The Trouble angel rolled his eyes dramatically. "Of course not. But it's no worse than the endless dithering you're doing now. I mean, how hard is it to make a decision? You're an adult, right?"

Adam shook his head, frustration bubbling up. "This is my family we're talking about. It's not a joke."

Angel Adil smirked. "Oh, lighten up. You know what they say: 'When in doubt, do nothing and hope it all works out on its own.'"

Adam couldn't help but laugh at the absurdity of it. "You're the worst angel ever."

The Trouble angel put his hands behind his head, looking pleased with himself. "That's the spirit! Embrace the chaos. Makes life more interesting."

Adam sighed, feeling a strange mix of exasperation and amusement. "So, what's your brilliant advice for handling this situation?"

Trouble angel pretended to think deeply, tapping his chin with exaggerated seriousness. "Let's see... How about you ignore all medical advice, go on a spontaneous road trip, and let fate decide? Or better yet, binge-watch a TV series and pretend none of this is happening."

Adam chuckled despite himself. "You're not exactly helpful, are you?"

Angel Adil grinned. "Nope. But I'm fantastic at making bad ideas sound good."

As the sarcastic angel continued to poke fun at his predicament, Adam felt a strange sense of relief. Trouble angel's ridiculous suggestions and sarcastic remarks, though utterly unhelpful, provided a bizarre distraction from the gravity of his situation.

It was as if the absurdity of it all made his burden just a little bit lighter.

"You know," Angel Adil said, leaning in conspiratorially, "sometimes, doing the wrong thing can lead you to the right place. Or it can lead to utter disaster. Either way, it's entertaining."

Adam shook his head, smiling despite his better judgment. "You're impossible."

Trouble angel stood up, stretching theatrically. "And you're still here, still indecisive. Maybe you should try flipping that coin after all. It might be the most decisive thing you've done all day."

As the Trouble angel sauntered off to explore the house, making sarcastic comments about Adam's choice of décor and the dust on the shelves, Adam realized that, despite the angel's unorthodox approach, he felt a bit better. Sometimes, a little humor, even from a sarcastic Trouble angel, was what he needed to face the overwhelming choices ahead.

Adam sat back on the couch, shaking his head. "Alright, Angel Adil". Let's see what other bad advice you've got. Maybe you'll accidentally stumble onto something useful."

Adil grinned widely. "Now that's the spirit! Let the chaos commence!"

Chapter 5 - The Surgeon

Dr. Isabella Martinez sat in her dimly lit office, the soft hum of fluorescent lights overhead providing the only sound apart from her own steady breathing. She had spent the last several hours poring over test results, scans, and medical charts, her mind working tirelessly thinking of the operation for Stephanie and the baby. The situation had escalated in the past few days, and now, the odds were stacked against them.

The hospital director, a tall, stern man with a thick gray beard, had just left her office after a tense discussion. He had reiterated the urgency of the situation, stressing that if Stephanie's condition worsened, they would need to operate immediately to avoid losing both mother and baby. He insisted that she push Adam to make the ultimate decision—a decision that no one should ever have to make.

Isabella, known as Dr. Isabella to her colleagues, was a serious and successful surgeon. Originally from Mexico, she had spent most of her life in the United States, graduating at the top of her class and becoming one of the best surgeons in her field. She was known for being tough and direct with her staff to the point of being rude and was not liked by many.

Dr. Isabella leaned back in her chair; her eyes closed as she rubbed her temples. She has a twin sister, Maria, who is critically ill and in desperate need of a heart transplant. The news that Stephanie was a match for Maria had added a layer of complexity and anxiety to an already dire situation. She only had one thought on her mind, that if Stephanie is not going to make it, she needs to secure the heart donation for her sister.

As she sat there, grappling with her thoughts, Bella's mind wandered back to her childhood in Mexico. She and Maria had always been inseparable, sharing everything from toys to secrets. The bond between them was unbreakable, and the thought of losing her twin was unbearable. Maria's illness had brought them even closer, and Bella had devoted herself to finding a way to save her sister. Now, she found herself at a crossroads, torn between her duty as a doctor and her love for her sister. As a matter of fact, she lied to Adam about his wife's condition and that Stephanie actually has very high chances to survive. The thought of losing her twin sister was unbearable and pushed her to make such a wrong decision, modifying a patient report in the system to make it look like she has no chance of survival, which is not only unethical but also a crime that will lead to her death.

That evening, Bella returned home, her heart heavy with the weight of her ethical dilemma. She sought solace in her favorite hobbies, cooking and drinking wine. As she chopped vegetables and sipped a glass of red, her mind raced with conflicting thoughts. The smell of garlic and onions filled the kitchen, but even the familiar comfort of cooking could not soothe her soul.

Later that night, as Bella sat in her living room, a presence made itself known. She felt a shiver run down her spine as she looked up to see her guardian angel standing before her, glowing with a soft, comforting light. But alongside the guardian angel was another figure—a dark, menacing version of herself, her trouble angel.

Bella was in shock; she screamed and ran to her bedroom in fear. The two angels followed her to the room and cornered her. She could not breathe and could not move. She was trembling.

The Trouble angel sneered; her eyes filled with malice. "Hi I am Angel Barbil, you know what you have to do, Dr. Isabella. Save the baby and secure Stephanie's heart for Maria. It's the only way to save your sister."

Bella's guardian angel placed a gentle hand on her shoulder. "And I am Angel Bella, you know in your heart what is right. You cannot sacrifice one life for another. You must find a way to be true to your ethics."

But her trouble angel was relentless, her voice dripping with venom. "Don't listen to her. Think of Maria. She's your sister, your twin. You can't let her die when you have the power to save her."

Bella was terrified. She ran away from the figures, her heart pounding in her chest. "This can't be real," she whispered, her voice trembling. "I must be hallucinating."

In a panic, she ran to the phone and dialed the emergency line. "Please, I need help. There are intruders in my house," she said, her voice frantic. "I think I'm hallucinating, but I can see them. They're still here."

The operator assured her that help was on the way. Bella hung up, her hands shaking as she glanced back at the angels. The guardian angel remained calm, while the trouble angel smirked.

Minutes later, the sound of a siren filled the night, and Bella's front door was flung open by a police officer. He was a tall man with a stern face, his hand resting on his holstered weapon. "Ma'am, are you alright? Where are the intruders?"

Bella pointed towards the angels; her voice shaky. "They're right there. I can see them. They're talking to me."

The officer looked around the room, his brow furrowed in confusion. "Ma'am, there's no one here. Are you sure you're not imagining things?"

Bella's eyes filled with tears. "I'm not crazy. I swear I saw them. They're right here."

The officer's face softened as he saw her distress. "Ma'am, have you been drinking or under a lot of stress lately? Sometimes that can make you see things that aren't there."

Bella nodded, her shoulders slumping. "I've been under a lot of pressure. I'm so sorry. I must be hallucinating." At this moment the angels had disappeared, and Bella was calmer.

The officer gave her a sympathetic look. "It's alright, ma'am. Try to get some rest and take care of yourself. If you need anything, don't hesitate to call." After the officer left, Bella sat on the couch, her body trembling. She could still feel the angels, and the fear in her eyes was evident.

Minutes later, they showed up, and the guardian angel approached her, speaking in a soothing voice. "Isabella, you are not crazy. We are real, and we are here to help you. You have a difficult decision to make, and we are here to guide you." Bella's guardian angel asked her to calm down and explained the entire angelic experience.

Bella's breathing slowed as she listened, her fear slowly dissipating. "I don't know what to do. I feel so lost." The guardian angel smiled gently. "Trust in yourself, Isabella.

Bella wiped away her tears; her heart still heavy, she whispered. "I'll try to do what's right." Bella knew that the journey ahead would be challenging. Deep down in her heart, she knew she was lying to the guardian angel. Deep down, she can only see saving her sister no matter what. The love for her sister and seeing her suffer were overwhelming and pushed her to make such a difficult choice.

Chapter 6 - The Meeting

Emilia stood outside Stephanie's hospital room along with her angels, who cannot be seen by anyone except her, her heart racing as she hesitated before entering. She wasn't sure why she had come here, maybe she was looking for answers and a way out to save her future husband. Taking a deep breath, she pushed open the door and stepped inside. The room was dimly lit, filled with the soft hum of medical equipment. Emilia's eyes fell on Adam, who was sitting beside Stephanie's bed, holding her hand as if it were the only thing keeping him grounded. His own angels stood there as well, not seen by Emilia.

Adam looked up, startled by her entrance. Emilia froze, feeling suddenly out of place. "Oh, I'm sorry," she stammered, feigning surprise. "I must have the wrong room. I was looking for my mom's room." Angel Malika leaned towards her and said with a smile, "Not a bad lie, Emilia."

Adam's tense expression softened, and he managed a faint smile. "It's alright. These hospitals can be confusing."

Emilia nodded, but instead of leaving, she found herself lingering by the door. There was something in Adam's eyes—an exhaustion, a despair—that tugged at her heart. "I... I can go, but you seem like you could use someone to talk to," she said softly, surprising even herself with the offer.

Adam looked at her for a long moment, as if weighing her words. Then, he nodded, his voice barely above a whisper. "Actually, that would be nice. I'm Adam, by the way."

"Emilia," she replied, stepping further into the room and closing the door behind her. "We can stay for a bit, if that's okay with you." She stumbled and said, "I mean, I." After all, she needs to totally ignore her angel's presence; otherwise, people will think she is crazy.

Adam nodded again, his grip tightening on Stephanie's hand. "I could use the company. It's been... a lot."

Emilia moved closer and took a seat beside him, feeling a strange sense of connection as they began to talk. It was as if fate had led her to this moment, and she couldn't shake the feeling that their lives were about to become even more intertwined.

Adam felt so comfortable opening up to Emilia, who seemed like a loving and caring person. He told her the entire story of the hit and run till reaching this moment. He expressed that the hit-and-run person cannot be found or identified. He shattered their lives and disappeared. Emilia felt shivers down her spine as she heard Adam talk about her Sam. While she felt the relief that no one could identify him, she felt the guilt building on and on. If she could just tell him the truth, if she could just ask for forgiveness, but it's not possible, at least not at this time.

Before they could say more, the door swung open, and Dr. Isabella entered the room. Her expression was serious, her steps purposeful. Emilia couldn't help but notice the slight tension in the doctor's posture, the way her eyes flicked between Adam and Stephanie with a calculating gaze. As with Emilia and Adam, Dr. Isabella walked in with her two angels not seen by others.

This is the first time they all gathered in one room, and they did not know it. Each of them has his own angels by him. The angels could not see each other at this point, and they kept quiet in this awkward moment, waiting to see what would happen next.

"Adam," Dr. Isabella began, her voice steady but urgent, "we need to talk about Stephanie's condition. Time is running out, and a decision must be made soon."

Adam's grip on Stephanie's hand tightened. "What do you mean, Dr. Isabella? What decision?"

Dr. Isabella took a deep breath, her face softening slightly, though there was a hard edge to her tone. "Stephanie's condition is deteriorating rapidly. The baby's life is in serious danger, and the longer we wait, the more we risk losing them both. We need to consider performing an emergency C-section to save the baby."

Adam's eyes widened in horror. "But what about Stephanie? What happens to her if we do this?"

Dr. Isabella hesitated, her gaze briefly shifting away from Adam. "The chances of Stephanie surviving the procedure are extremely low. The surgery would put a tremendous strain on her already weakened body. If we proceed, we're likely to lose Stephanie, but we might be able to save the baby."

The words hung in the air like a death sentence. Adam stared at Dr. Isabella, disbelief and panic etched across his face. "You're asking me to choose between my wife and my child," he whispered, his voice breaking.

Emilia felt a surge of sympathy for Adam, her own heart aching at the impossible choice he was being forced to make. She stepped closer to him, placing a gentle hand on his shoulder. "Adam, I can't imagine what you're going through right now".

Adam looked up at Emilia, his eyes filled with desperation and helplessness. "I don't know what to do. How can I possibly make this choice? How can I choose between the love of my life and our unborn child?"

Dr. Isabella, sensing the urgency of the situation, pressed forward. "Adam, I understand how difficult this is, but we don't have much time. Every minute we wait puts both of them at greater risk. We need to make a decision soon, or we could lose them both."

Emilia could see the strain in Dr. Isabella's face, the way her hands clenched at her sides as if she were holding back something more. There was a cold determination in the doctor's voice that unsettled her, but she couldn't place why. It felt like there was more at play here, something beyond the immediate medical crisis.

Adam's head fell into his hands, his shoulders shaking with silent sobs. Emilia knelt beside him, wrapping her arms around his trembling form.

Dr. Isabella's eyes flickered with something unreadable as she watched the interaction between Emilia and Adam. "Adam," she said, her voice softening just a fraction, "I know this is a terrible choice to have to make, but you need to consider the future. If we save the baby, Stephanie's legacy will live on. Your child will have a chance at life, a chance to carry on her memory."

Adam looked up at Dr. Isabella, his face a mask of anguish. "But what if Stephanie could survive? What if there's a chance, she could make it?"

Dr. Isabella's expression grew more serious, her tone firm. "Adam, I have to be honest with you. The chances of Stephanie surviving are slim to none. If we try to save them both, we could end up losing both of them. I need you to think about what Stephanie would want, about what's best for your child."

Emilia could see the conflict raging within Adam, the way his eyes darted back and forth as if searching for an answer that wasn't there. She tightened her grip on his shoulder, her voice gentle but resolute. "Adam, whatever you decide, you have to trust yourself. You know Stephanie better than anyone. You know what she would want."

Adam's eyes filled with tears as he looked at Emilia, his voice barely above a whisper. "She would want our baby to live. She always talked about how much she wanted to be a mother. But I don't know if I can live without her."

Dr. Isabella nodded; her expression somber but resolute. "It's an impossible choice, Adam. But you have to make it. For your child's sake."

Emilia watched as Adam struggled with the weight of the decision, her own heart breaking for him. She could see the turmoil in his eyes, the fear and the grief. She wished she could take some of that burden from him, but she knew this was a choice only he could make. After what felt like an eternity, Adam inquired when this decision had to be made, and Dr. Isabella gave him 48 hours.

As Dr. Isabella left the room, Emilia remained by Adam's side, her heart heavy with the enormity of the decision he had just made. She knew this was only the beginning of the pain and heartache that lay ahead, but she was determined to be there for him, to help him through whatever came next.

"I'm here for you, Adam," Emilia whispered, her voice thick with emotion. Adam looked at her, his eyes filled with a mixture of gratitude and despair. "Thank you, Emilia".

As Emilia walked out of the hospital, the weight of the situation bore down on her like a heavy cloak. The crisp air outside did little to alleviate the suffocating pressure in her chest. Her steps were slow and deliberate as she reached for her phone, her fingers trembling slightly as she dialed Sam's number. The familiar sound of his voice on the other end brought her no comfort this time.

"Sam," she began, her voice strained and barely above a whisper, "I need to tell you something. The accident... the one you were involved in... it's not just about us anymore. Someone's going to die because of it."

There was a long pause on the other end, and Emilia could hear the sharp intake of breath as Sam struggled to process her words. She didn't wait for his response, couldn't bear to hear his voice, filled with guilt or denial. Instead, she continued, her words tumbling out in a rush.

"I just left the hospital. There's a man, Adam... his wife, Stephanie, she was in the van you hit. She's dying, Sam. And now he's being forced to choose to save the baby and let his wife die within the next 48 hours. This is all because of that night."

Emilia's voice broke as she spoke, tears streaming down her face. "I can't keep this inside anymore, Sam. You need to know what's happening. We need to figure out what to do, how to make this right, because this... this is on us now."

Silence hung heavily between them, and Emilia could only hear the sound of her own ragged breathing. She waited, hoping for something—anything—from Sam, but all she heard was the overwhelming weight of the truth they could no longer escape.

Chapter 7 - The Confession

Emilia awoke the next morning with a heavy heart, the weight of the previous day's events pressing down on her like a suffocating blanket. The thought of returning to the hospital gnawed at her, but she knew she had no choice. Adam needed her, and she couldn't abandon him now, not when he was on the brink of making the most agonizing decision of his life. But she couldn't do it alone. She needed someone by her side, someone who could offer support and strength where she felt herself crumbling. That's when she decided to bring Jennifer along.

As they drove to the hospital, Emilia remained silent, her mind racing with conflicting thoughts. The presence of her angels, invisible to Jennifer, was a constant reminder of the secret she harbored. How could she face Adam, knowing that Sam—the man she loved—was the reason for his unimaginable pain? But she had to push those thoughts aside for now. Today wasn't about her guilt; it was about helping Adam through this impossible situation.

Jennifer sensed the tension in Emilia and tried to lighten the mood. Emilia managed a weak smile, grateful for Jennifer's unwavering support. "Thanks, Jenny. I really need you today."

When they arrived at the hospital, Emilia took a deep breath before leading Jennifer to Stephanie's room. Adam was sitting in the same spot as before, his eyes weary, his face pale with exhaustion. He looked up as they entered, offering a faint smile.

"Adam, this is Jennifer," Emilia said, introducing her friend. "She's my best friend and assistant, and I thought she could help us figure things out."

Adam nodded, the weariness in his eyes giving way to a flicker of hope. "It's nice to meet you, Jennifer. Thank you for being here."

Jennifer smiled warmly, taking a seat beside Emilia. "Of course, Adam. I'm here to help in any way I can."

As they began to talk, Emilia noticed something strange happening in the corner of the room. Her angels, who usually remained close to her, had moved to the side and seemed to have their own deep conversation. Their expressions were serious as they observed the humans in the room.

Adam, unaware of the angelic meeting taking place, continued to pour out his heart, sharing his fears and doubts with Emilia and Jennifer. He felt an odd sense of comfort in their presence, as if the weight of his decision was slightly easier to bear with them by his side.

After spending time at the hospital, Emilia and Jennifer eventually left, promising to return the next day. But for Adam, the turmoil was far from over. Back at home, the silence of his empty house was suffocating. His guardian angel stood by his side, while Angel Adil lingered nearby, smirking.

"I don't know what to do," Adam muttered, running a hand through his hair. "I need to save them both. There has to be a way."

The guardian angel's voice was calm but firm. "Adam, I cannot intervene directly. I can only offer guidance. The decision lies with you, and you must trust yourself to make the right one."

Adam's frustration boiled over. "But how can I choose? I feel like I'm going crazy, seeing you, talking to you like this. Is any of this even real?"

Angel Adil chuckled, his voice dripping with sarcasm. "Real or not, you're stuck with us. So why not just roll the dice and see what happens?"

Adam ignored the trouble angel, his desperation growing. He grabbed his phone and dialed Emilia's number, needing her calming presence, her advice.

Emilia answered on the first ring; her voice filled with concern. "Adam? What's wrong?"

"Can you come over? I... I need help. I don't know what to do."

Without hesitation, Emilia agreed, and within an hour, she and Jennifer were at Adam's apartment. As they settled into the living room, the atmosphere was thick with tension. Adam's angels hovered nearby, watching silently, while Emilia's angels stood close to her, their expressions unreadable.

Adam struggled to find the words, glancing nervously at his angels. Finally, he blurted out, "I see them." The angels. They're here, right now."

Jennifer's eyes widened in surprise, her gaze darting around the room as if trying to spot the invisible beings. "Angels? Adam, what are you talking about?". Jennifer starred at Emilia's eyes in shock and wondered "could this be the same, could Adam see his angels like Emilia?"

Adam's voice shook as he continued, "I know it sounds crazy, but they're real. They've been with me ever since... since the accident. I don't know what to do. I'm losing my mind."

Emilia, her heart aching for him, reached out and took his hand. "You're not crazy, Adam. I see them, too."

Adam's eyes widened in disbelief. "You do?"

Emilia nodded, tears welling up in her eyes. "Yes, I do. I've been seeing them for a while now. And they're here to help us, to guide us through this."

Jennifer, still trying to process everything, looked between them, her expression one of disbelief mixed with concern. "Okay, so... Do both of you see angels? And they're here with us right now?"

Before anyone could respond, a cool breeze swept through the room, causing them all to shiver. The air seemed to hum with an electric energy, and suddenly, Emilia gasped as she saw Adam's angels for the first time. Standing across from them, Adam stared in shock at Emilia's angels, now visible to him as well.

Jennifer's eyes widened as she looked around the room, and for the first time, she saw the four angels standing before them. Her mouth opened in a silent scream, and then everything went black as she fainted.

"Jenny!" Emilia cried out, rushing to her side.

They managed to wake Jennifer after a few moments, and as she regained consciousness, she looked around in disbelief. The angels were still there, watching them with calm expressions.

"What... what just happened?" Jennifer whispered, her voice trembling.

Angel Mila stepped forward, her voice soft and soothing. "Do not be afraid. Because Emilia and Adam have acknowledged each other's visions, they can now see each other's angels. And because of your close bond with Emilia, you have been granted the ability to see us as well."

The revelation left them all stunned, but there was little time to process it. Mila's trouble angel "Malika" spoke up, her voice laced with a hint of mischief. "Well, isn't this a fun little gathering? All of us here together—what are the odds?"

Adam's guardian angel, his tone serious, addressed the group. "This moment is significant. The next phase of your lives will be crucial. The decisions you make now will shape your future, for better or worse."

Adam, still in shock, turned to Emilia. "Why are your angels here? What's your story?"

Emilia hesitated, the truth weighing heavily on her heart. She glanced at Jennifer, then back at Adam. "It's... related to my family. There's a lot I need to tell you, but not tonight. We'll talk about it soon, I promise."

As the weight of the situation began to settle over them, they all moved to sit in a circle in the living room. The tension slowly began to ease, the surreal nature of the evening giving way to a strange sense of camaraderie.

Jennifer, ever the pragmatist, finally broke the silence with a nervous laugh. "So... angels, huh? I guess I really need to start watching what I say."

She reached out a hand towards Emilia's guardian angel, her curiosity piqued. Her fingers passed through the angel's form, causing Jennifer to jump back in surprise.

The guardian angel smiled gently. "We are not flesh and blood, Jennifer. When the time is right, we will disappear."

Jennifer, regaining her composure, couldn't resist making a joke. "So, you're saying I can't ask you to help with the dishes?"

The Trouble angels chuckled; their voices filled with sarcasm. "Oh, we'd be terrible at that. But we can offer some hilariously bad advice if you're interested."

The group shared a laugh, the tension easing as they realized they were in this together, angels and all. As the night drew to a close, they agreed to take things one step at a time, to support each other as they navigated the strange and challenging road ahead.

Before they parted ways, Emilia's guardian angel spoke one last time, her voice filled with quiet strength. "Remember, you are never alone. We are here to guide you, but the choices are yours to make."

Jennifer looked back at Adam, held his hand tightly and told him she will visit the hospital to meet with Dr. Bella and discuss with her Stephanie's case one more time and the options available before making a final decision. In her mind she even thought to have a second opinion from another surgeon before proceeding.

As they left Adam's apartment, the weight of the evening's revelations hung over them, but so did a sense of newfound resolve. They didn't know what the future held, but they knew they would face it together, with their angels by their side.

Chapter 8 - The Turning Point

The sun dipped below the horizon as Emilia sat in her car, gripping the steering wheel with knuckles that turned white. The day's revelations had left her deeply shaken. She had shared a connection with Adam deeper than she ever anticipated—one that was now entwined with the unseen forces of their angels. She could no longer escape the truth. Her role in this web of tragedy loomed over her, and the weight of her silence felt unbearable.

Her Trouble angel "Malika", lounging in the passenger seat, broke the silence. "You're overthinking this, Emilia," she said, inspecting her nails as though the situation were nothing more than an amusing inconvenience. "Why ruin what's left of your life? If you confess, you'll destroy not just yourself but everyone around you. Ever thought of that?"

"Stop," Emilia snapped, her voice trembling with barely suppressed anger. "I've heard enough."

The Trouble angel raised an eyebrow, her smirk widening. "Oh, have you? Let me guess. That goody-two-shoes guardian angel is whispering sweet nothings in your ear about redemption and truth? Let me tell you something, sweetheart: truth doesn't set you free. It chains you down."

From the back seat, Angel Mila stepped forward, her serene expression unwavering despite the turmoil. "Emilia, you must not let fear dictate your actions. The truth may hurt, but it is necessary. Healing cannot begin until the lies are uncovered."

The two angels' voices rose, each trying to drown out the other, and Emilia pressed her hands to her temples. "Enough!" she shouted, the sound echoing in the enclosed space. Her breath came in short, shallow gasps. She had never felt more torn.

Deep down, she knew her guardian angel was right. She couldn't keep this secret forever. But the fear her Trouble angel invoked—the image of Adam's devastation, of Sam's fury—kept her paralyzed.

By the time Emilia reached home, her nerves were frayed. She opened the door to find Sam sprawled on the couch, scrolling through his phone. He glanced up at her and immediately noticed her strained expression.

"Hey," he said, setting his phone down. "You, okay? You look... stressed."

Emilia hesitated, unsure where to start. The words felt heavy in her throat, and she struggled to meet his gaze. "Sam, we need to talk."

He sat up straighter, concern clouding his features. "What's going on?"

Emilia took a deep breath and began recounting the events of the past few days—the angels, her connection to Adam and his family, the accident, and the devastating decision Adam now faced. Her voice trembled as she described how her angels had become visible and how Adam had seen his own, as well as Jennifer seeing all of them. She spoke of the moral crisis they were all entangled in, the weight of which was suffocating her.

When she finished, Sam's face was a mask of disbelief. He stood, pacing the room with a nervous energy. "Emilia, listen to yourself. Angels? Shared visions? This... this is insane. Are you hearing what you're saying?"

"It's real, Sam!" Emilia insisted, her voice rising. "I see them. Adam sees them. Even Jennifer does now. This isn't in my head."

Sam stopped pacing; his arms crossed tightly over his chest. "You're exhausted. You've been under a lot of pressure, and it's messing with your mind."

Emilia's frustration boiled over. "Stop dismissing me! You think I'm making this up? Do you think I want this? Do you have any idea how terrifying it is to see and hear things no one else can?"

Sam's face softened slightly, but he still shook his head. "I don't know what's going on with you, Emilia, but I can't believe this. Angels aren't real. Whatever you're seeing—it's not normal."

Emilia's heart sank. She had hoped Sam would understand, that he would stand by her. "Fine," she said, her voice trembling. "Then come to the hospital with me. Meet Adam. See what's happening for yourself."

Sam hesitated, visibly uncomfortable. "The hospital? Emilia, I don't think that's a good idea."

"It's not about what's good for us," Emilia said, her tone firm. "It's about what's right. Adam needs support, and we owe it to him to be there."

Sam rubbed the back of his neck, avoiding her gaze. "Let me think about it."

Meanwhile, at the hospital, Dr. Isabella sat in her office, her hands trembling as she stared at the falsified medical reports. Her guardian angel "Bella" stood silently in the corner, radiating calm, while her trouble angel "Barbil" leaned against the desk with a smug expression.

"You're running out of time, Isabella," Angel Barbil said, her tone almost sing-song. "Tick-tock. Either you save your sister, or you let her die. Simple math."

Angel Bella stepped forward. "Dr. Martinez, you must listen. If you proceed with this plan, there will be consequences you cannot foresee and this path will lead to disaster."

Bella clenched her fists, her mind racing. She thought of her twin sister, Maria, lying in a hospital bed, her life slipping away.

She couldn't bear the thought of losing her. "I don't have a choice," she whispered, her voice cracking.

"You always have a choice," the guardian angel said gently. "But you must consider the greater good."

Angel Barbil rolled her eyes. "The greater good? Oh, please. You're a surgeon, Bella. Save your sister. That's all that matters."

A knock on the door startled Bella out of her thoughts. She quickly hid the reports as Jennifer entered, her expression determined.

"Dr. Martinez," Jennifer said, her tone polite but firm. "I'm here to discuss Stephanie Adam's case. Adam wants a second opinion, and I'll need access to her medical records."

Bella's heart skipped a beat. She forced a calm smile. "I'm afraid hospital policy doesn't allow me to release records without proper authorization."

Jennifer wasn't deterred. "Adam is willing to sign the consent form. I'll have it to you by the end of the day."

Bella felt panic rising. If those scans and records were reviewed by another doctor, the falsifications could be exposed. Her trouble angel smirked, whispering in her ear, "You're running out of excuses, Bella. Better come up with a plan."

"Of course," Bella said, her voice tight. "But I assure you, we're doing everything we can for Stephanie."

Jennifer's gaze was piercing. "I'm sure you are. But Adam deserves peace of mind. I'll be back with the form."

As Jennifer left, Bella slumped in her chair, her trouble angel "Barbil" cackling softly. "Better think fast, Doc. The clock's ticking."

The guardian angel remained silent; her sorrowful gaze fixed on Bella. Deep down, Bella knew she had crossed a line, and the path forward was growing darker with each passing moment.

Emilia and Jennifer reconvened in the hospital cafeteria, the weight of the day's events pressing heavily on them. Jennifer relayed her conversation with Dr. Isabella and her reluctance to release Stephanie's records.

Emilia nodded, her stomach twisting. "We need to get those records and get a second opinion for Adam's sake. The only way to save Sam from this mess is if they both come out alive, Emilia said.

Jennifer placed a comforting hand on Emilia's shoulder and looked at the angels standing near them, shaking her head. As they prepared to leave, Angel Mila whispered softly, "The truth will come to light, Emilia, and I am very happy with how you have been handling this situation."

Emilia glanced at her trouble angel, who lounged nearby with a mocking grin. "Or," Malika said with a smirk, "you could just let it all burn. Makes for a better story."

Emilia closed her eyes, steeling herself. The turning point was upon them, and she had no choice but to face it head-on.

Chapter 9 - The Angelic Conclave

The night was still, with the moon casting a cold, pale glow over the city. Emilia, Adam, and the others slept fitfully, their minds burdened by the weight of the drama that consumed their lives. But as the humans wrestled with their inner demons, their angels gathered for a fateful meeting.

In a hidden realm just beyond the human eye, the four angels appeared—two glowing with the soft luminescence of hope and righteousness, and two cloaked in shadows, their forms flickering with mischievous, chaotic energy. The space they inhabited seemed infinite yet intimate, a neutral ground where both light and shadow mingled uneasily.

Angel Mila stepped forward, her radiant form pulsing with determination. Her voice was calm but firm, resonating with authority. "We must talk. The situation has gone too far."

Angel Malika, smirked as she lounged against an invisible barrier, her dark form casually exuding defiance. "Oh, here we go. Another lecture about morality, I assume? Can't wait to be inspired."

"Enough," said Angel Adam, his presence steadier and older, like a sturdy oak amidst a storm. He glanced at all the angels with a mix of patience and frustration. "The humans are at a breaking point. They are confused, lost, and teetering on the edge of decisions that will change their lives forever. This is not a game."

Adam's trouble angel "Adil" clapped mockingly, his grin sharp and wolfish. "Oh, bravo. A moving speech. But you're forgetting something, old-timer—we live for these moments. This is the game, and we're winning."

"You mistake chaos for victory. There is no triumph in destruction. The lives we are meant to guide hang in the balance, and your meddling could lead to irreversible consequences," said Angel Mila.

Adam's trouble angel "Adil" rolled his eyes dramatically. "Blah, blah, blah. Irreversible consequences, moral high ground—don't you ever get tired of your self-righteous babbling? It's exhausting."

The tension in the air thickened, and the luminescent glow of the guardian angels seemed to intensify as they faced their shadowy counterparts. Angel Mila raised a hand, her expression unyielding. "This is not the time for mockery. The humans need clarity, not confusion. Our purpose is to guide them toward their better selves, not to drag them further into chaos."

Angel Malika leaned forward, her dark eyes glinting with mischief. "Your purpose? Oh, sweetie, our purpose is just as important. Humans are complicated. They need to see their darker sides, confront their fears, and embrace their flaws. That's where we come in. Without us, they'd be boring little robots."

Adam's Trouble angel "Adil" nodded enthusiastically. "Exactly. You guardians want them to be perfect saints, but that's not how the world works. A little chaos never hurt anyone."

"That's where you're wrong," Angel Adam said sharply. "This isn't about imperfection. It's about choices. And your interference isn't helping them grow; it's keeping them from facing the truth."

The Trouble angels exchanged amused glances, as if they found the guardians' arguments naïve. "Oh, please," Emilia's Trouble angel said, her voice dripping with sarcasm. "Let's not pretend the truth is some magical cure-all. The truth can destroy them. Sometimes lies and chaos are kinder."

"That's a coward's justification," Angel Mila retorted, her voice rising with an intensity that sent ripples through the ethereal space. "The truth might be painful, but it is the only path to healing. It is what they need to confront their fears and move forward."

The argument reached a boiling point as all four angels began speaking over one another, their voices clashing like thunder and lightning. The guardians pleaded for reason and righteousness, while the trouble angels reveled in their defiance, championing chaos and doubt.

Finally, Angel Mila stepped between the two groups, her voice cutting through the cacophony. "Enough!" she commanded, her presence commanding attention. "We are not here to quarrel. We are here because the humans' lives are at a crossroads, and the choices they make will shape not just their futures but the futures of those around them. If we allow our disagreement to fester, we fail them all."

The Trouble angels fell silent, though their expressions remained defiant. Angel Malika tilted her head, her grin returning. "Alright, Ms. Noble. What's your brilliant solution, then?"

"We challenge you," Angel Mila declared, stepping forward. Her voice was resolute, her glowing form almost blinding in its radiance. "Let the humans' choices decide. We will guide them toward honesty, redemption, and healing. You will push them toward fear, chaos, and destruction. And in the end, their decisions will reveal whose influence is stronger."

The trouble angels exchanged wary glances. For all their bravado, they knew the stakes were high. "Fine," Angel Malika said, folding her arms. "But don't cry when your precious humans disappoint you. They always do."

"Humans are capable of great things," Angel Adam replied firmly. "Even in their darkest moments, they have the strength to choose the light. You'll see."

"Let's make this interesting, then," Angel Adil said, a wicked gleam in his eye. "Winner gets bragging rights for eternity."

The guardian angels remained unfazed; their resolve was unshaken. "We don't need to win," Angel Mila said quietly. "We need them to find their way."

With that, the conclave dissolved. The angels returned to their respective humans, each carrying the weight of the night's confrontation. The guardians were filled with hope and determination, while the trouble angels retreated with gleeful anticipation, ready to sow seeds of doubt and confusion.

But one thing was certain: the battle between light and shadow was far from over, and the humans' choices would determine who ultimately prevailed.

Chapter 10 - The Conspiracy

The moon hung low, casting an eerie glow over the quiet city streets. In the unseen realm, hidden just beyond human perception, the Trouble angels convened once more. Their meeting ground was an ethereal, shadowy domain, pulsating with a sinister energy that seemed to echo the chaos they thrived on. Despite their spectral forms, their presence exuded an overwhelming sense of malice and purpose.

"Well, well," Angel Malika, Emilia's trouble angel, purred, her dark eyes glinting with malevolent excitement. She stood with her arms crossed; her posture relaxed yet radiating an air of dominance. "I'd say we're making excellent progress, wouldn't you?"

Adam's trouble angel "Adil" smirked, leaning casually against an invisible barrier, his aura flickering with a mischievous energy that betrayed his eagerness. "Progress? Darling, this isn't just progress. This is art—a tapestry of despair woven with the finest threads of doubt and manipulation."

Dr. Isabella's Trouble angel "Barbil" appeared in a ripple of shadowy energy, his grin sharp and predatory. His movements were deliberate, like a puppet master carefully inspecting his strings. "I have my own masterpiece to contribute. Bella's resolve is weakening, but a nudge here, a little lie there... she'll do what needs to be done. She won't even realize how deep she is in until it's too late."

The three trouble angels "Malika, Adil and Barbil" huddled closer together, their conspiratorial whispers filling the space with an electric tension. Each of them was eager to share their schemes, to take pride in the chaos they had sown, and to devise new ways to tighten their grip on the humans they influenced.

Angel Barbil took center stage in their planning. "Bella is teetering on the edge," she began, her voice a low, hypnotic murmur that resonated in the empty void around them. "All she needs is a push—a reminder of what's at stake. Tonight, I'll convince her that waiting any longer will cost her sister's life. She'll have no choice but to falsify the records further, ensuring no one suspects a thing."

Angel Adil leaned in, his expression gleeful and calculating. "And I'll work on Adam. He's already drowning in guilt and fear. It won't take much to convince him that saving the baby is the only way to honor Stephanie's memory. He's vulnerable— his love for Stephanie makes him pliable."

Angel Malika, Emilia's shadowy counterpart, laughed softly, her voice dripping with mockery and dark amusement. "And sweet Emilia... She's a bundle of nerves already. She's torn between guilt and obligation. I'll make sure she stays focused on convincing Adam to make the 'right' choice. And as for her precious Sam? I'll keep him sidelined long enough to ensure his guilt keeps him from interfering. He'll only show up when it's too late to change anything. The tangled web they'll all be caught in will be exquisite."

The three Trouble angels exchanged a triumphant look before dispersing, each setting off to execute their part of the devious plan. Their laughter echoed in the void, a sound that reverberated with malevolent glee.

Late that night, Dr. Isabella sat alone in her dimly lit office, the faint hum of fluorescent lights overhead providing the only sound apart from her unsteady breathing. She leaned back in her chair, staring at the stack of medical records before her. Stephanie's file lay on top, its stark black-and-white printouts detailing a grim prognosis. Bella's fingers trembled as she tapped them against the edge of her desk, her mind racing with conflicting thoughts.

Angel Barbil appeared without warning, his presence casting an oppressive shadow over the room. He leaned against the desk, his form shifting subtly like smoke caught in a breeze. "Bella," she whispered, her voice smooth and persuasive. "Time is slipping away. Every second you hesitate brings Maria closer to death."

Bella didn't respond immediately. She stared at the file, her throat tightening. "I know," she finally whispered, her voice cracking. "But falsifying these records further... it's wrong. If anyone finds out—"

"No one will find out," Angel Barbil interrupted, her tone firm yet comforting. She stepped closer, leaning in as though sharing a dark secret. "You're not just a doctor; you're a sister. Isn't it your duty to save Maria? To do whatever it takes?"

Bella's shoulders slumped, and her hands fell to her lap. Her trouble angel could see the hesitation in her eyes, the inner turmoil that threatened to consume her. She capitalized on it, her voice softening into a coaxing lull. "Think of Maria's smile, her laughter. Think of the years you've shared. Are you really willing to let that slip away because of a stranger who, let's be honest, has no chance of surviving?"

The words struck a chord deep within Bella. Her fingers tightened into fists, and her jaw clenched. The trouble angel leaned back, satisfied that her seeds of doubt were taking root. Bella slowly reached for Stephanie's file, her hands trembling as she began altering the records. Her Trouble angel watched with satisfaction, her grin widening as Bella sealed her fate.

Meanwhile, Adam sat alone in Stephanie's hospital room, the rhythmic beeping of monitors providing a grim soundtrack to his despair. He sat slouched in a chair, his head in his hands, his mind consumed by a storm of guilt and helplessness. Every memory of Stephanie—their laughter, their plans for the future—seemed to mock him now, reminding him of what he stood to lose.

Angel Adil materialized silently, his presence barely noticeable save for the subtle chill that settled over the room. He took a step closer to Adam, his voice low and insidious. "She's slipping away, Adam," he murmured, his tone heavy with false sympathy. "But you have the power to make her sacrifice mean something. Save the baby. It's what Stephanie would want."

Adam lifted his head slightly, his red-rimmed eyes gazing blankly at the wall. "I don't know if I can," he muttered, his voice hoarse. "I feel like I'm betraying her."

"You're not betraying her," the trouble angel countered, his words laced with an almost hypnotic cadence. He crouched down beside Adam, speaking softly yet urgently. "You're honoring her. She dreamed of being a mother, Adam. Let her dream live on through your child. It's what she would have wanted."

Adam closed his eyes, his hands gripping his hair as though trying to hold himself together. Angel Adil words resonated with him, planting seeds of doubt and guilt that began to take root in his heart.

Across the city, Emilia sat on the edge of her bed, her hands gripping the sheets as though they were the only thing tethering her to reality. Her mind raced with conflicting thoughts, each one more suffocating than the last. Angel Malika lounged nearby; her dark form draped across the room's shadows like a silk curtain. She exuded a smug confidence, her presence both unsettling and magnetic.

"You can't let Sam get involved," Angel Malika said, her voice a mixture of sarcasm and urgency. "If he shows up, everything falls apart. You'll lose him, Emilia. And you'll go down with him for covering up the accident."

Emilia pressed her hands against her temples, her chest tightening as anxiety clawed at her. "But I can't keep lying to Adam," she said, her voice barely above a whisper. "He deserves the truth."

Angel Malika rolled her eyes dramatically, sitting upright as though the suggestion physically pained her. "Oh, spare me. The truth will ruin everything. Focus on convincing Adam to save the baby. That's the only way out of this mess. One clean decision, and you'll be free."

The internal struggle was evident in Emilia's tear-filled eyes. She knew Angel Malika words held a twisted logic, but the thought of lying further made her stomach churn. Still, Angel Malika's relentless whispers continued to erode her resolve.

The next morning, Jennifer arrived at the hospital early, her steps purposeful as she carried Stephanie's records which she collected earlier from her hospital. She had sent them to a trusted friend, Dr. Raymond, for review and was anxious to hear his thoughts. By noon, she received the results: the records confirmed Dr. Isabella's assessment—Stephanie's condition was critical, and saving the baby was the best viable option.

Jennifer rushed to Adam's room; her expression somber as she approached him. Emilia sat beside him, her hand resting on his arm in silent support. "Adam," Jennifer began gently, her tone cautious yet firm. "I had another surgeon review Stephanie's case. They agree with Dr. Isabella. If we wait any longer, we'll lose them both."

Adam's face crumpled, and he let out a choked sob, his shoulders shaking as the weight of the decision crushed him. Jennifer wrapped her arms around him, whispering soothing words as tears streamed down her own face. The weight of the decision was unbearable, but the manipulated records left them no choice.

Emilia sat on the chair outside Stephanie's room, the weight of the decision pressing heavily on her chest as she dialed Sam's number with trembling fingers. The room felt colder, as if the gravity of what she was about to say had sucked all the warmth from the air. When Sam answered, his voice was weary, carrying the burden of sleepless nights and unresolved guilt. Emilia took a deep breath, her voice shaking as she began to speak. She explained in halting words that the surgery was scheduled for the next morning at 7 AM, and the decision had been made to save the baby at the cost of Stephanie's life. She could hear the sharp intake of breath on the other end of the line, a sound laden with shock and shame.

Emilia pressed on, her tone resolute despite the tears welling in her eyes, urging Sam that it was time for him to confront the consequences of that fateful night. She told him that Adam needed support—someone to stand by him in his moment of unimaginable grief—and so did she. Her words were both a plea and a challenge, calling Sam to face not only the man whose life had been shattered but also the weight of his own actions. The line was silent for a moment, filled only with the distant hum of background noise, before Sam finally spoke. His voice was low and filled with remorse, agreeing to come to the hospital.

Emilia could sense the deep conflict within him, a mix of guilt, fear, and a reluctant acceptance that he owed it to Adam, Stephanie, and their unborn child to be there. As she ended the call, Emilia felt a faint glimmer of relief amid the turmoil; for all his faults, Sam was willing to face the truth.

That night, the Trouble angels gathered once more in their shadowy domain, their laughter echoing like a chorus of malevolence. Angel Malika, raised an invisible glass in mock toast. "We did it," she said, her voice dripping with satisfaction. "Everything's in place. Tomorrow, chaos reigns."

Angel Adil grinned, his aura pulsating with anticipation. "And the guardians? Clueless. They'll never see it coming."

Angel Barbil nodded in agreement, his expression one of smug triumph. "By this time tomorrow, Stephanie will be gone, the baby will be born, and the fallout will be delicious."

The three Trouble angels reveled in their success, confident that the stage was set for the ultimate upheaval. Tomorrow would bring a reckoning—one that would forever alter the lives of those they sought to manipulate.

Chapter 11 – Goodbye Stephanie

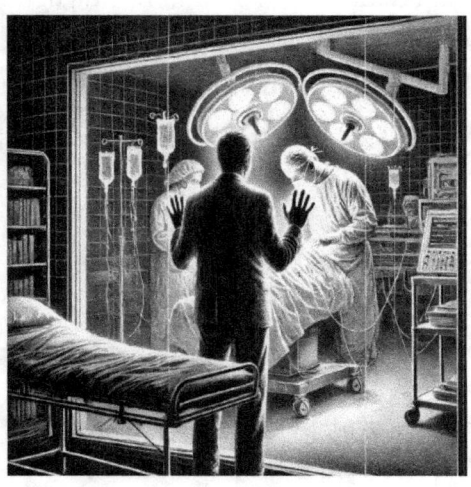

The operating room was shrouded in an eerie stillness, broken only by the rhythmic beeping of the monitors. Adam stood behind the glass window; his palms pressed against the cold surface. His heart raced, but he forced himself to stay upright. The last words he had whispered to Stephanie echoed in his mind: I love you. Whatever happens, I'll keep our baby safe.

Inside, Dr. Bella worked with meticulous precision. The surgical lights illuminated Stephanie's pale, fragile body, a stark contrast to the vibrant woman she had been. Every incision and movement were deliberate and calculated. Bella's assistant handed her the necessary tools without a word, the gravity of the moment weighing on the entire team. But within Dr. Isabella, a storm raged—a battle between the ethical boundaries she had crossed and the personal loyalty driving her actions. Stephanie's life hinged on Bella's decision, which she could never reverse.

Outside, Adam's emotions collided like waves against jagged rocks. Emilia sat beside him, her hand resting lightly on his arm, offering silent comfort. Beside her stood Sam, stoic and distant, his guilt building walls around him. Jennifer was there too, occasionally whispering words of reassurance to Adam, though her own anxiety made her voice tremble.

Adam turned to Emilia, his eyes hollow, his voice a broken whisper. "What if I made the wrong decision? What if I just sentenced my wife to death?"

Emilia squeezed his arm, her heart aching for him. "You didn't. You chose what she would have wanted. She would want your baby to live, Adam. You know that."

Suddenly, a nurse burst into the waiting area, her expression grim. "Mr. Adam?"

Adam shot to his feet, Emilia and Jennifer standing with him. Sam hung back; his jaw tight.

"The baby is stable and breathing on her own," the nurse said quickly, her tone professional but strained. "However, your wife..." She hesitated, and Adam's chest constricted.

The nurse's lips pressed together, her eyes softening with sympathy. "I'm so sorry. We did everything we could, but Stephanie didn't make it through the procedure."

The words slammed into Adam like a sledgehammer. His knees buckled, and Jennifer caught him, guiding him to a chair. He clutched his head in his hands, a raw, guttural cry tearing from his throat.

"No, no, no," he repeated, rocking back and forth. "This can't be real. She can't be gone."

Emilia knelt beside him, her own tears falling freely. She didn't have words—there were no words for this kind of pain. All she could do was hold his hand and let him grieve. Sam sat there watching all the unfolding events and feeling more and more guilt. He thought he literally killed Stephanie by his recklessness, something that cannot be undone. He cried and cried.

Hours later, in another part of the hospital, Dr. Isabella stood in the transplant unit. Stephanie's heart, still strong and vibrant, was now being prepared for Bella's sister, Maria. As the transplant team worked, Bella lingered in the shadows, her chest tight with a mixture of relief and guilt.

Maria had been brought into the operating room earlier that day. Now, as Bella watched the team prepare to save her sister's life, she whispered a silent prayer—for Stephanie, for Adam, for Maria, and for the morality she had set aside to make this happen.

"It's done," one of the surgeons said to Bella hours later, pulling down his mask. "The heart is a perfect fit. Maria's vitals are strong."

Bella's knees nearly gave out. She steadied herself against the wall and nodded. "Thank you," she said softly, her voice strained.

But the relief was short-lived. As Bella walked away from the operating room, she caught sight of Adam down the hall, sitting in a chair, his face buried in his hands. Emilia sat beside him, holding the newborn baby girl wrapped in a pink blanket. Bella's steps faltered. For the first time, she felt the weight of her decision settle heavily on her shoulders. She'd saved her sister, but at what cost?

"She's beautiful," Emilia whispered, gazing down at the baby in her arms. The little girl's tiny fingers curled into a fist, her chest rising and falling with soft breaths.

Adam looked up; his face streaked with tears. "She's all I have left of Stephanie," he said, his voice cracking. "I don't even know how to do this. How can I be a father when I'm broken?"

Emilia placed the baby gently in his arms, her touch lingering for a moment. "You'll learn. Because she needs you. And Stephanie would want you to be strong for her."

Adam stared at the baby, his heart aching with both love and grief. "Her name is Lily," he said softly, the name catching in his throat. "Stephanie always wanted to name her Lily."

Jennifer, standing nearby, wiped her tears and offered a soft smile. "Lily it is. She's lucky to have a dad like you, Adam. And we're here for you. Every step of the way."

Sam, who had remained mostly silent, finally stepped forward, his expression conflicted. "You're not alone in this, Adam," he said quietly. "We'll do whatever it takes to help."

Adam nodded, his gaze never leaving his daughter. "Thank you," he murmured, though his voice was distant. His grief was still raw, but the small, fragile life in his arms gave him a reason to keep going.

The days that followed were a blur for Adam. Arrangements for Stephanie's funeral were made, and Lily was cared for by Emilia and Jennifer while Adam grappled with his grief. But one thing burned fiercely in his heart: finding the driver who had caused the accident.

"The police need to do more," Adam told Emilia one evening, his voice filled with frustration. "They can't let this go unsolved. Stephanie deserves justice."

Emilia's stomach churned, her guilt growing heavier with each passing day. She nodded, unable to meet his gaze. "They'll find him, Adam. They're doing everything they can."

But Emilia knew the truth. She knew the driver was Sam, the man she loved. The weight of her silence was suffocating her, and it was beginning to show.

Meanwhile, Sam's own guilt was eating away at him. He avoided Adam as much as possible, claiming work obligations, but Emilia saw the cracks in his composure.

"I can't keep this up," Sam said one night, pacing their living room. "Every time I see him, I feel like I'm going to explode."

"We'll figure it out," Emilia said, though her voice lacked conviction. "We just need to give it time."

Sam stopped pacing and looked at her, his eyes filled with desperation. "Time isn't going to fix this, Em. I cannot look Adam in the eyes every day. It's killing me"

In the quiet corners of their lives, the Trouble angels reveled in the chaos they had sown. But the guardian angels were not idle. They watched closely, ready to intervene when the time was right, their quiet strength a beacon amidst the storm of emotions. They knew that the road ahead would be fraught with pain and hard choices, but they held faith in their charges, believing that redemption and healing were still within reach.

The days following Stephanie's passing were a blur of grief and hollow routine. Adam sat alone in the nursery, staring blankly at the crib where his newborn daughter slept soundly, unaware of the world's tragedies. The walls of the room were painted in soft yellows—Stephanie's favorite color—and every inch of it carried her touch. The sheer silence of her absence weighed like a boulder on his chest.

Adam's guardian angel stood behind him, a solemn presence bathed in soft light. "She is safe, Adam," the angel whispered. "Stephanie's love lingers here, in every corner, in every breath of your child."

Adam clenched his fists, his voice a broken whisper. "Did I make the right choice?"

Angel Adil materialized beside him, its shadow curling like smoke around the room. "Right? Wrong? Such human words," it sneered. "You chose, and now you suffer the consequences. That is all."

Adam shut his eyes tightly, as though willing away the conflict raging in his soul. Despite the newborn's soft cries and the angels' presence, he felt utterly alone.

Emilia sat on the edge of her bed, staring at her trembling hands. Stephanie's death had shaken her deeply. The memory of Adam's face as he crumbled under the weight of loss replayed in her mind over and over. A part of her wanted to confess everything to him—the accident, her and Sam's guilt—but her Trouble angel "Malika" perched on the windowsill, weaving webs of doubt.

"Tell him? Ruin everything? You think he can handle the truth?" Trouble angel's voice dripped with mockery. "You'll lose everything... his friendship, your peace, and Sam."

"Stop it," Emilia murmured, her voice weak. "I need to do the right thing."

Angel Mila stepped forward, its golden glow pushing back the shadows. "The truth will hurt, but it will set you free, Emilia. Trust yourself."

Tears burned Emilia's cheeks as she covered her face with her hands, trapped between the pull of light and darkness.

Sam spiraled. He hadn't been to work in days, and his phone buzzed incessantly with calls he ignored. Beer cans littered his apartment, and he sat slouched on the couch, staring at nothing. Guilt gnawed at him like a relentless parasite.

When Emilia finally showed up at his door, she gasped at the sight of him.

"Sam, you... You can't keep doing this," she whispered.

He looked up at her with empty eyes. "Doing what? Living? I killed someone, Emilia. What's the point anymore?"

"It wasn't all your fault," she said, though the words felt hollow.

His gaze hardened. "What do you want me to do? Turn myself in? Destroy everything I have left?"

"You have to face this, Sam. We both do."

Sam shook his head and looked away. "You do what you want, Emilia. Leave me out of it."

That night, Emilia sat alone in her car outside his building, her heart breaking. Her Trouble angel whispered, "He's not the man for you. You know it." By the next morning, she made her decision. She broke up with Sam.

Meanwhile, Jennifer was torn apart by what is happening to her friend Emilia. She wants to support but does not know how. She also felt so bad for Adam, who was torn apart just losing the love of his life and now stuck alone with his newborn baby. She has a good heart and fell in love with the baby since she was born. She showed up at Adam's door, and with a big smile, she said, "How are you, Papa?" I am here to hang out with you and the baby. Adam put on a big smile and welcomed her to his apartment. During the past weeks they grew closer to each other, and Jennifer felt so comfortable hanging out with him.

He sighed. "You don't have to do this." Jennifer shook her head, a small, knowing smile on her lips. "I want to. You shouldn't have to do this alone, Adam."

Her words hung in the air between them, soft yet heavy with unspoken meaning. Adam looked at her then, really looked at her, as though seeing her for the first time. She was no longer just the friend who stepped in to help; she was someone who anchored him to life when everything else felt adrift. He noticed the gentle way she cradled the baby, the kindness in her eyes, and the quiet strength that never wavered, even when his own resolve faltered.

As time passed, the moments they shared grew longer, more intimate. A quiet understanding passed between them; a bond forged not just through shared grief but through the fragile hope of rebuilding something new. One evening, after putting the baby to sleep, Jennifer found Adam sitting on the floor beside the crib, his back against the wall, his head bowed. She crouched beside him, her hand resting on his arm.

"You're doing so well," she said softly. "Stephanie would be proud."

Adam lifted his head, his eyes glistening. "I... I don't know what I'd do without you, Jennifer."

Her fingers lingered against his arm as she smiled gently. "I am here because I want to be here, and I feel good to be here," she said.

Something shifted between them in that moment, a spark igniting where only shadows had lingered before. Adam reached out, brushing a strand of her hair back behind her ear, his hand lingering against her cheek. Jennifer froze, her breath catching, but she didn't pull away. Their eyes locked, and the silence between them became charged with something deeper—something fragile and beautiful that neither dared name.

Tentatively, Adam leaned forward, and Jennifer closed the space between them. Their lips met in a kiss—soft, hesitant, but filled with a tenderness that both surprised and overwhelmed them. It was a kiss born of shared sorrow and newfound connection, a quiet promise that maybe, just maybe, they could find solace in each other.

When they pulled apart, Jennifer's cheeks flushed, and Adam looked at her with a mixture of awe and uncertainty. "I... I'm sorry," he murmured, as though afraid he had crossed a line.

Jennifer shook her head, her voice barely above a whisper. "Don't be."

Neither of them spoke after that, but the air between them felt different, electric yet comforting. Jennifer stood and held out her hand, pulling Adam to his feet. They didn't need to say anything more; the moment spoke for itself. That night, as Jennifer quietly left the house, Adam watched her from the doorway, a strange mix of hope and guilt flickering in his chest. For the first time in a long time, the emptiness didn't feel so absolute.

Chapter 12 – The Angel World

Beneath the ethereal glow of the twilight stars, a congregation of both guardian and trouble angels convened within a secluded grove, the air thick with the anticipation of a celestial council. The atmosphere was charged, a palpable tension weaving between the illuminated forms of the guardians and their darker counterparts.

Angel Malika, flanked by Barbil and Adil, hovered slightly above the ground, her smirk conveying a triumph that felt out of place in the sacred quiet of their meeting space. "Our gambits have yielded fruit," she declared, her voice tinged with a dark glee. "We nudged, we pushed, and we watched as the mortals danced to our discordant tune."

Barbil, with a nod, added, "The good doctor was especially responsive. A little push, and she crossed lines she never thought she would. It's fascinating what fear and desperation can do to a human."

Adil laughed, a sound that echoed ominously through the grove. "And let's not forget how beautifully Adam crumbled under the weight of grief and responsibility. Such exquisite despair!"

The guardians listened, their luminous forms dimming with each confession. Angel Mila, her expression etched with sorrow and disbelief, stepped forward. "How could you celebrate this?" she implored, her voice rising in a crescendo of anguish. "We are meant to guide, to illuminate the path of righteousness and hope, not to lead them into darkness!"

The Trouble angels paused, the flickering shadows around them seeming to pulse with their laughter. Malika tilted her head, considering Mila's distress. "Guide? Illuminate? Dear Mila, we merely exposed the depths of their souls. We showed them what lurks in the shadows of their hearts. Isn't self-awareness a gift?"

"No," Mila countered sharply, her aura flaring with a brilliance that momentarily illuminated the grove. "You manipulated, you coerced, and you led them astray. What happened to the tenets we uphold? To the balance we are sworn to maintain?"

The debate that followed was heated and intense, with the guardians expressing their shock and dismay at the extent of the trouble angels' interference. The core of their discord lay in the fundamental differences in their approach to their duties.

"It went too far," Mila finally said, her voice heavy with the weight of their collective failures. "The damage is too much. This isn't guidance; it's destruction."

A heavy silence settled over the group, the severity of the situation sinking into every celestial heart present. It was clear that the actions of the Trouble angels had spiraled beyond the realm of mere influence into something far darker.

"We need counsel," Mila stated, her decision ringing with the authority of her ancient wisdom. "This matter must be brought before the Chief of Angels. We must seek wisdom from above, to discern the path forward and to restore the balance that has been so grievously upset."

The other guardian angels nodded in agreement; their expressions somber. They all looked to Mila, whose resolve had always guided them through celestial storms.

"I will go," Mila volunteered, her voice steady despite the turmoil that churned around them. "I will ascend to the heavens and bring our plea to the Chief of Angels. This cannot continue. We must right what has been wronged."

With a final glance at her counterparts, whose smirks had faded into thoughtful frowns, Mila spread her wings, which shimmered with the light of a thousand stars. As she ascended, the remaining angels, both guardian and trouble, watched her rise into the sky, her form gradually disappearing into the celestial expanse.

Below, the world of humans remained oblivious to the cosmic debates over their fates, caught up in their own terrestrial struggles and heartaches. But above, in the realms where light battles shadows, a plea for intervention was winging its way to the highest authority, carrying hopes for redemption and a return to equilibrium.

The Angels' World unfolded above the mortal plane, a realm where the skies shimmered with infinite hues and the air resonated with a celestial melody. Here, in this boundless expanse, angels thrived in a harmony unimaginable to human minds. The skies were an endless expanse, a tapestry woven with radiant orbs of light that drifted like stars, each one a living beacon of hope and purpose. Towering crystal palaces hovered amidst floating islands, their surfaces reflecting the golden light of countless radiant orbs that danced like stars. The very air seemed to hum with an energy that could be felt deep within the soul, a symphony that played without beginning or end, resonating with the essence of the universe itself.

Each angel bore a unique form, reflecting their roles and their innermost essences. The guardian angels, ever luminous and warm, emanated an aura of peace and protection. Their features were both serene and resolute, their translucent wings shimmering with iridescent hues that seemed to ripple like water under sunlight. The Trouble angels, in contrast, embodied an interplay of shadow and light, their forms dynamic and enigmatic, their eyes reflecting the complexities of human choices. These angels were no less radiant, but their brilliance was tempered by an air of mystery and challenge, as if they carried the weight of the universe's untold stories.

Two distinct regions defined the Angels' World, each tailored to the needs and purposes of its inhabitants. The Guardian Haven was a sanctuary of radiant light, where streams of energy cascaded like waterfalls, nourishing the spirits of the guardians. The land seemed to pulse with life, its crystalline structures glowing softly, and its pathways paved with starlight. Here, their leader presided with wisdom, ensuring that their efforts aligned with the higher purpose of maintaining harmony on Earth. The Haven was a realm of solace, where soft fields of starlight provided rest for weary angels, and the air itself was imbued with a serenity that eased even the most burdened hearts.

On the other side, the Shadows cape served as the dwelling for Trouble angels. This realm was neither dark nor foreboding but brimming with shifting energies. The skies above the Shadows cape churned with swirling patterns of light and shadow, reflecting the duality of the Trouble angels' nature. Rivers of stardust twisted in unpredictable patterns, their currents echoing the unpredictability of human struggles. The Trouble angel's leader commanded a space of constant motion, encouraging his followers to challenge stagnation and inspire growth through adversity. The Shadows cape was a realm of transformation, where every corner held the potential for revelation, and every shadow concealed a spark of light.

Both realms converged at the Higher Council of Angels, the heart of the celestial domain. This sacred space floated amidst the cosmos, an awe-inspiring construct of interwoven energy and light. Its foundations seemed to be woven from the very fabric of the universe, shimmering with a brilliance that defied comprehension. It was here that the Chief of Angels presided. Surrounding him were the council's advisors, their forms radiating unparalleled brilliance. The Council's setting was a symphony of cosmic beauty: moons, suns, and constellations moved in perfect synchrony, forming an ever-changing backdrop of celestial wonder. This was a place where decisions of cosmic importance were made, where the balance of the universe was weighed and maintained.

Emilia's guardian angel "Mila" arrived at the higher council, her luminous form standing out even among the radiant advisors. The council's entrance, a grand archway of spiraling light, opened to welcome her as she stepped into the sacred hall. Awaiting her was the chief advisor, whose calm demeanor and commanding presence set the tone for the gathering. He pulsed softly as he extended a greeting, his voice resonating with a warmth that immediately put her at ease.

She explained the imbalance that had begun to threaten the human world, detailing how certain trouble angels had failed to uphold their role. Chaos had proliferated without the intended purpose of growth, and if left unchecked, this imbalance could spiral into widespread disaster. The advisor's expression faltered, a rare display of surprise. He assured her that the chief himself would hear her plea and that immediate steps would be taken. These particular trouble angels would cease their direct influence over humans until the council reached a resolution, a decision made by the advisor and a measure meant to stabilize the precarious balance between light and shadow. With this decision the trouble angels disappeared at once and can no longer be seen.

Meanwhile, on Earth, the absence of the trouble angels brought a strange stillness to those they had once influenced. Adam, now adjusting to his new life as a father, found comfort in the presence of Jennifer and his guardian angel. The angel's gentle guidance helped Adam embrace the challenges of parenting, and as days turned into weeks, a deeper bond formed between him and Jennifer. Together, they navigated the intricacies of raising the child, their shared purpose drawing them closer.

Adam's once uncertain heart now found solace in the quiet moments spent with his child, the warmth of Jennifer's presence becoming a beacon of hope in his life.

For Emilia, the disappearance of her angels left her disoriented. Days passed without their familiar presence, and she began to wonder if their absence signified an end to their guidance. At the bank, she went through the motions of work, her once sharp focus dulled by a lingering sense of unease. She avoided Sam, the weight of their shared secret growing heavier with each passing day. Emilia's once vibrant spirit seemed dimmed, her laughter infrequent, and her thoughts often consumed by the choices she had made and the truths she had yet to confront.

Driven by curiosity and concern, Emilia visited Adam's house one evening. She was greeted by Jennifer, whose warmth momentarily eased Emilia's apprehension. Inside, Emilia saw Adam's guardian angel watching over him, a quiet but constant presence. She hesitated before speaking, noting the angel's steadfast vigil but wondering aloud why the trouble angels were absent. Adam's guardian angel turned to her, his light pulsing softly. He explained that the trouble angels had been withdrawn, citing an imbalance that required higher intervention. Emilia's heart quickened as she realized the gravity of the situation, her mind racing with questions she dared not voice aloud. This is when Emilia inquired to why her guardian Angel "Mila" can no longer be seen and Angel Adam explained that she is on a celestial mission and will be back in sometime.

In the hospital, Dr. Isabella's recovery from nervous breakdown was slow but steady. Her guardian angel remained by her side, offering quiet encouragement as she grappled with the consequences of her actions. One evening, as she stared out of her hospital window, the angel spoke gently to her about regret and redemption. The doctor's thoughts turned to her trouble angel, whose absence she now noticed acutely. She muttered bitterly about the influence they had over her, but her guardian angel reminded her that the decisions had always been hers alone. Redemption, they explained, begins with accepting responsibility. Bella's heart ached as she pondered the words, a seed of hope taking root amidst the rubble of her remorse.

In the celestial skies, the Higher Council of Angels convened. Emilia's guardian angel stood before the chief and the advisors, her plea echoing in the vast, luminous hall. The celestial bodies surrounding the council moved in harmonious orbits, casting an otherworldly glow over the gathering. The chief's voice resonated with the authority of countless ages, assuring that the imbalance would be addressed. He welcomed Emilia's guardian angel to the council and requested her to tell the facts.

She explained the imbalance that had begun to threaten the human world, detailing how certain trouble angels had failed to uphold their role. Chaos had proliferated without the intended purpose of growth, and if left unchecked, this imbalance could spiral into widespread disaster. Trouble angels, once vital players in the dance of human choice, had strayed from their purpose. Instead of subtly influencing humans to reflect and learn from their hardships, they had imposed their will, steering decisions to serve their ends. Such direct interference disrupted the delicate equilibrium that allowed free will to flourish. Humans, robbed of genuine choice, became pawns in a game of unchecked influence, their paths diverted from growth toward a cycle of confusion and conflict.

The council chamber filled with a hushed resonance as they listened. The chief of angels reminded everyone that the role of angels was not to dictate but to guide—to serve as subtle whispers in the storm of human consciousness. The misuse of such influence by trouble angels was an affront to the sacred balance of existence. Human decisions, while flawed, were essential to the natural order. To tamper excessively with these choices was to unravel the very fabric of growth and learning that defined life.

The debate deepened as more council members entered the discussion. The Chief of Angels, his form a beacon of timeless wisdom, acknowledged the gravity of the situation. The council deliberated on the profound interplay between light and shadow, good and bad. It was not enough to merely eliminate darkness, the chief emphasized; growth emerged from the friction between the two. Trouble angels had a purpose, but their current actions skewed that purpose, creating ripples of imbalance that threatened not just humanity but the cosmic harmony that bound all existence.

Arguments arose about whether angels, even trouble angels, should wield the power to sway humans so definitively. Some advisors argued that humans, gifted with free will, should never face influences so potent that their autonomy was compromised. Others contended that hardship and temptation were vital teachers, provided they remained within the bounds of subtlety. Direct intervention, as seen in recent events, undermined the integrity of choice itself, reducing humanity's struggles to preordained outcomes rather than genuine trials of character.

Emilia's guardian angel interjected; her voice steady but impassioned. She spoke of the humans she had guided, of their capacity for resilience when left to navigate their paths with only the gentlest nudges from above. She described how interference—be it from guardians or trouble angels—diminished the authenticity of their journeys. Humans needed room to decide, to stumble, to rise from their failures, for it was in those moments that they discovered their strength.

The chief listened intently. He acknowledged that the trouble angels' actions, while rooted in their purpose of challenging humanity, had crossed into manipulation. It was a delicate balance, he mused. Angels were never meant to decide outcomes but to inspire decisions, to illuminate paths without choosing them. He assured the council that this imbalance would not go unchecked. He confirmed the decision of the advisor that those trouble angels would cease their direct influence over humans until the council reached a resolution, a very needed temporary measure.

As the chamber filled with celestial light, Angel Mila felt a renewed sense of purpose. She trusted that the council's wisdom would prevail and that light, tempered by understanding and guided by humility, would ultimately restore the equilibrium necessary for both humanity and the cosmos to thrive. The council decided to go into private deliberation and come back with decisions.

What came next was a surprise to everyone. The council reconvened again under the supervision of the chief of angels, who stood high above the council members and advisors to share the council's decision.

The Chief of Angels decided to uphold a higher court gathering to include all guardian and trouble angels, not only this, but also invite the humans to the hearing. He explained that without listening to humans' point of view they can't make a good decision, and for this to work with out impacting the balance on earth, humans will be invited during their dreams to the council and when they wake up, they will not remember anything of what has transpired. Angel Mila was shocked as she did not know this is possible but she was very excited that the council would hear directly from the humans.

The next evening during the early hours of the night all guardian angels were summoned to the council along with trouble angels, awaiting the start of the unprecedented trial.

Chapter 13 - The Council

The celestial hall echoed with a faint hum; a sound reminiscent of countless wings brushing softly against the unseen expanse of the skies. It was an unprecedented gathering—one that even the oldest angels in the council could not recall in their immortal memories. The Chief of Angels, regal and radiant, stood at the center, his towering form cloaked in an aura of golden light. With a commanding wave of his hand, he signaled the beginning of the session.

"Fellow guardians, watchers, and advisors," his voice resonated, warm yet commanding, "we gather today for a matter of immense importance. Events in the human realm have shaken the balance we are sworn to maintain. It is time for clarity, judgment, and, above all, understanding."

The council chamber, an infinite expanse of light and shadow, began to fill with the murmur of angelic voices. Seated to the right were the council members, their expressions solemn, while the advisors sat to the left, their postures reflective and inquisitive. In one corner, Angel Mila, Angel Adam and Angel Bella exchanged uneasy glances, their wings shifting as if to suppress the growing tension. Across from them, the trouble angels watched with a mix of curiosity and indifference, their darkly shimmering forms a stark contrast to the guardians' radiance.

The chief raised a hand, and silence blanketed the space. "This council has never before invited the mortal realm into our deliberations. Humans have been shielded from our presence, meant to imagine and believe until the day they face the ultimate truth. But now, the time has come to bring them here— not in body, but in spirit. Through their dreams, they will join us, unaware of this truth upon waking."

Gasps rippled through the chamber. One of the advisors, a sage angel with silvery wings, leaned forward. "Chief," he inquired, his voice measured but edged with skepticism, "how can this be done? The humans are bound to their earthly existence. Their souls cannot perceive our realm while they live."

The chief's expression remained serene. "In dreams, they can transcend their limitations. Dreams bridge realms, allowing mortals to see what they cannot comprehend while awake. Here, they will speak their truths and bear witness. It is essential to hear from all sides if we are to decide the future of humanity and preserve the balance of life."

A murmur of assent followed, though pockets of unease lingered among the gathered angels. The chief continued, his voice now firm with resolve. "Prepare yourselves", the celestial skies will transform to host this meeting. The humans will appear in the open expanse, visible and audible to us all."

He gestured to the skies above, and with a flick of his fingers, the chamber shifted. The infinite expanse now mirrored the earthly realm, with the vibrant blue and green orb of Earth suspended in the center. To its right, the moon emerged, glowing faintly. The sun appeared above, casting a warm, steady light, while the planets of the human solar system aligned to the left, each radiant with celestial energy. The stage was set.

Angel Mila, seated quietly in her corner, felt her wings tremble. The weight of her decisions and her presence here bore down on her. Yet, she remained confident that this was where she was meant to be, even as the uncertainty of what was to come lingered.

At last, the chief turned to the head advisor. The elder angel stood, his presence commanding respect. His voice, though quiet, carried the wisdom of eons. "The Divine has created a system that thrives on balance," he began, his tone steady. "We angels were crafted to observe, to guide, and to record. Not to interfere with free will, for that is the gift given to mortals. Humanity, intelligent yet flawed, is a testament to the beauty of choice. They weave their fates, reaping what they sow. Our role is not to direct but to illuminate and preserve the natural order. Today, we gather not to decide for them but to ensure fairness, to correct what has gone astray, and to hear the voices of all involved."

The council listened intently, the gravity of his words sinking in. The celestial stage now pulsed with anticipation, the vast audience of angels—both guardian and trouble angels—awaiting the historic moment when humans and angels would finally intersect.

With a commanding flick of his wrist, the chief motioned to the open skies. The atmosphere shifted, an interplay of light and shadow creating an otherworldly ambiance. "It is time," he announced. "Prepare to meet the mortals."

In the center of the skies, a faint shimmer appeared. Gradually, the forms of three humans emerged: Emilia, Adam, and Dr. Isabella. They floated, ethereal and dreamlike, their expressions reflecting the surreal nature of their arrival. Around the edges of the council, the angels whispered in awe. For the first time, mortals stood in their sacred realm, unknowingly bearing witness to the celestial world.

The chief stepped forward; his radiance dimmed slightly to avoid overwhelming the fragile human spirits. "Welcome," he said, his tone gentle but commanding. "Though you do not know it, you stand at the crossroads of destiny. Here, we shall speak of choices, of actions, and their consequences. You are safe and among those who wish to preserve the balance of your world. Listen well and speak true, for your voices matter."

The humans, though visibly confused, nodded as if compelled by an inner understanding. The celestial audience watched in silence; the weight of the moment heavy in the air.

The head advisor rose again, his presence filling the chamber. "This is a trial of truths," he declared. "The divine power watches over all, but today, the voices of mortals and immortals will intertwine to shape the path forward. Let us proceed with wisdom, grace, and fairness."

The celestial and mortal worlds had converged, their boundaries blurred in this moment of unity. All present—angel and human alike—felt the gravity of the unprecedented event. The council's proceedings began, a delicate dance of light and shadow that would determine the course of humanity and the fragile balance of existence itself.

The celestial chamber shimmered with an otherworldly glow; its vast expanse filled with rows of seats that seemed to stretch infinitely. At the heart of the chamber was the dais where the Chief of Angels sat, a figure of commanding presence whose eyes radiated both wisdom and authority. The atmosphere was heavy with anticipation as humans and angels alike gathered for an unprecedented trial—a confrontation to unravel the tangled threads of divine guidance and mortal autonomy.

The humans, Adam, Emilia, and Bella, stood at the center of the chamber, flanked by their respective guardian angels on one side and trouble angels on the other. The tension in the air was palpable. For the first time, they were brought together in this divine court, a place where truths would be laid bare and judgments made. The audience, composed of countless other angels, watched silently, their glowing forms radiating curiosity and unease.

The Chief of Angels, a towering being of light, raised a hand for silence. "This trial is of utmost significance," he declared, his voice echoing through the chamber like a symphony. "It concerns the delicate balance between divine intervention and human free will. Let the truth be revealed."

Emilia's guardian angel was the first to step forward, her glowing form exuding calm determination. "Chief," she began, her voice resonant and clear, "we, the guardian angels, have always strived to illuminate the path for our humans, ensuring they navigate life with clarity and purpose. However, the trouble angels have strayed from their duties. They conspired against their charges, leading to chaos and irreversible harm. Emilia abandoned her fiancé, Bella killed Stephanie, and Adam made a devastating choice, manipulated by lies and deceit."

Her words caused a ripple through the audience, their soft murmurs carrying an undercurrent of shock. The trouble angels, with their dark, brooding forms, exchanged glances before one of them, Angel Adil "Adams' Trouble Angel", stepped forward. His expression was defiant yet tinged with regret. "We preserved humanity's raw emotions," he said, his voice a low rumble. "Our interference was not out of malice but to ensure that they felt the full spectrum of their experiences. Without pain, joy is meaningless. Without a doubt, faith cannot be tested."

The humans, who had remained silent thus far, exchanged uneasy glances. Adam was the first to speak, his voice breaking with emotion. "You manipulated us," he accused, his gaze fixed on his trouble angel. "You filled my heart with doubt and fear when I needed clarity. You robbed me of my ability to make a choice freely, and now I live with the consequences of decisions that feel... less than my own."

Emilia stepped forward, her voice trembling but resolute. "We relied on you to guide us, not to control or deceive us. Free will is what makes us human. If our decisions are coerced, how can we grow? How can we learn?"

The chief of angels then called upon Angel Barbil "Isabella's Trouble Angel" and question him about his manipulation of Dr. Bella, which caused a human to kill another human. Angel Barbil admitted his wrong doing along with other trouble angels, but also expressed that showing up to humans and challenging the guardian angels caused this imbalance which created a ripple effect out of their control.

Dr. Isabella's voice was softer but no less impactful. "You showed us our worst fears, clouding our judgment. We deserve guidance, yes, but not at the expense of our agency." Dr. Bella continued "If you did not show up in my life, if you did not push me, if you let me think without interruption, maybe I would have made the right decision, you see humans after all are fragile beings and each one of us has a different level of strength and beliefs based on how we were raised. Some can be influenced more than others".

The chamber fell silent as the humans' words hung in the air. The Chief of Angels closed his eyes, his expression contemplative. "Guardian angels," he said, "do you affirm that your intentions have always been to illuminate the path without overriding free will?"

"We do," they replied in unison, their voices steady and unwavering.

The trouble angels, though hesitant, came forward as well. "We confess," Angel Malika said, her voice subdued. "We conspired, not out of malice but to challenge and test. Yet, we see now that our actions caused harm beyond what was intended."

The chief's gaze swept over the gathered assembly. "This trial reveals much about the complexity of our roles and the fragility of human autonomy. It is clear that both guidance and restraint are necessary. Angels must be companions, not overlords. Humans must be allowed to make their own choices, for it is through these choices that they learn and grow."

The humans, emboldened by the chief's words, addressed the crowd. Emilia spoke first; her voice filled with conviction. "We are flawed, yes, but our flaws make us who we are. We need your guidance, but we must own our decisions. To be truly human is to choose, without intervention, even if that choice leads to mistakes."

Emilia added, "If angels control our every move, we lose the essence of what it means to live. Free will is not just a gift; it is a responsibility we must bear, for better or worse."

Bella's words were a plea and a promise. "Help us when we need you, but let us find our own way. That is the only way we can truly grow."

The Chief of Angels raised his hands, his wings unfurling in a gesture of peace. "This trial has been enlightening. Let it be known that from this day forward, a new harmony shall be forged. Guardian angels shall resume their duties, guiding their charges while respecting their autonomy. Trouble angels will cease to appear to humans to avoid any further misguidance and allow the humans to make their own decisions and bring balance back to their lives. Once this situation is resolved, guardian angels as well will cease to appear directly to humans, guiding them only through dreams and subtle, subconscious means. The trouble angels who caused this situation will be punished."

The humans then asked, their voices tentative yet earnest, "Chief, how can we undo what has happened? Can we right the wrongs?" The chief's eyes softened as he responded, "Some wrongs can be mended, and others cannot. A life lost cannot be restored, but a lie can be corrected, and trust can be rebuilt. Redemption lies not in undoing the past but in seeking resolution and forgiveness. Your actions moving forward, guided by integrity and sincerity, will determine the healing of these wounds. Understand that while the past is unchangeable, your future remains unwritten."

A sense of resolution filled the chamber as the chief's words resonated. The humans, their faces lined with emotion, began to fade from the celestial realm. As they disappeared, their words lingered, a reminder of the fragile balance between guidance and free will.

When Adam, Emilia, and Bella awoke the next morning, they felt a profound sense of calm and clarity. Though they could not recall the trial, the presence of their guardian angels felt like a comforting reminder that they are not alone.

Chapter 14 – Back on Earth

The world continued to turn as the humans returned from the celestial trial, unaware of the monumental shifts that had taken place in their unconscious states. Guardian angels now stood resolutely by their charges, while trouble angels had been ordered to retreat into the shadows, their direct interference banned to ensure humans could make untainted decisions.

Emilia woke up early; her guardian angel gently explained the trial's results, emphasizing that the trouble angels had been mandated to step away. "Their presence," the angel said, "made humans feel obligated to act in ways they wouldn't naturally choose. You are free now, Emilia, to navigate your life without such undue influence."

The same morning, Adam sat in his nursery, staring at the crib where his infant daughter lay. He had decided to focus all his energy on being the best father he could be. Jennifer, always supportive, stood by his side as they grew closer, their shared grief gradually transforming into a bond of companionship and love. Emilia, sensing the need to rebuild her own life, spent more time with Adam and Jennifer. She became a trusted friend, often joining them for outings, dinners, and heartfelt conversations.

One afternoon, while they watched Jennifer play with the baby, Adam turned to Emilia. "I only saw your boyfriend once," he said casually. "During Stephanie's operation. Why hasn't he been around?"

Emilia hesitated, a lump forming in her throat. "Sam and I broke up," she admitted, trying to keep her tone light. "It was a personal decision." She didn't elaborate, and Adam didn't press her, sensing the subject's sensitivity.

Sam, meanwhile, struggled with Emilia's absence. His guilt and longing drove him to reach out to Jennifer, who had always been a mutual friend. "Can you help me talk to Emilia?" he asked her one evening. "I need to make things right." Jennifer agreed to mediate, seeing the pain in his eyes, but she warned him that Emilia would have conditions.

In the background, the police closed the hit-and-run investigation involving Stephanie's death. They had exhausted all leads and could not identify the runaway driver. Adam was disheartened, feeling that justice for Stephanie had been denied. The weight of unresolved loss sat heavily on his shoulders.

When Emilia finally agreed to meet with Sam, their conversation was filled with raw emotion. He admitted to his wrong doings, expressing his deep remorse. Emilia listened, her heart torn between her own pain and the possibility of forgiveness. "If we're to fix this," she told him firmly, "you need to come forward and admit the truth to Adam. He deserves that." Sam hesitated, fear clouding his face, but eventually nodded. "Give me some time," he pleaded. "I need to find the strength."

Emilia agreed, deciding to slowly prepare Adam for the truth. Her guardian angel stood by her side, offering silent encouragement.

The breaking point came during a dinner at Adam's home. Emilia, unable to bear the secret any longer, shared the truth. "Adam," she began hesitantly, her voice trembling, "there's something I need to tell you. My ex-boyfriend, Sam... he was the one who caused the accident. He's been wracked with guilt, and he wants to come forward and ask for your forgiveness."

Adam's face darkened as the words sank in. His expression twisted with disbelief, and for a moment, he sat frozen, as if his mind refused to process what he had just heard. Then, his voice broke the heavy silence, sharp and trembling. "You knew this all along?" he demanded, his eyes narrowing as they bore into Emilia's. The intensity of his tone sent a shiver through the room.

Emilia's voice cracked as she tried to explain. "I didn't know how to tell you. I thought—"

"You thought?" Adam cut her off, his voice rising. He turned to Jennifer, his breath uneven, as if he were struggling to contain his anger. "And you? Did you know?"

Jennifer's eyes welled with tears. She looked down at her hands, which trembled slightly as she clasped them tightly together. When she finally spoke, her voice was soft but laden with guilt. "I found out. I... I wanted to tell you, but I didn't know how. I was trying to find the right time, Adam, I swear."

Adam stood abruptly, his chair screeching against the floor as he pushed it back. The veins in his neck were taut, and his hands clenched into fists at his sides. His voice, when he spoke, was raw and broken. "So, you both kept this from me? You both decided it was okay to lie to me?" He turned back to Emilia, his gaze filled with anguish. "You knew what Stephanie meant to me, what this has done to me, and you still kept it quiet?"

Emilia's tears spilled freely now. "Adam, please, I didn't mean for it to happen this way. I... I wanted to help you."

"Help me?" Adam's laugh was bitter, a sound devoid of humor. "You call this help? You let me think I was surrounded by people who cared, who understood my pain, and all the while, you were hiding the truth from me."

He turned to Jennifer, his voice dropping to a hoarse whisper. "And you, Jennifer. I thought you loved me. I thought we were building something real. But now, it just feels like a lie. Were you even here for me, or was this all just some elaborate cover-up?"

Jennifer's tears streamed down her face as she reached out toward him. "Adam, please, it's not like that. I do love you. I was trying to figure out how to—"

"Enough," Adam snapped, his voice shaking with emotion. He stepped back, his chest heaving as he struggled to breathe through the storm of betrayal and grief that engulfed him. "Both of you... Just go. Get out of my house."

Emilia stepped forward, her voice trembling but steady. "Adam, you have every right to feel this way. But when you've had time to calm down, please let us talk again. You deserve the whole truth, and you deserve closure."

Adam didn't respond. His back was to them now, his shoulders rigid as he stared at the wall. Jennifer hesitated, her sobs choking her words, but she finally turned and fled the house. Emilia followed, her heart heavy with sorrow and guilt.

Next morning, Jennifer received a call from her doctor friend who had previously reviewed Stephanie's file. "Jennifer," the doctor said urgently, "I've been reviewing Stephanie's records, and there are some inconsistencies. Can we meet? I think there's something you need to know." Alarmed, Jennifer agreed and promised to investigate further.

At the hospital, Dr. Isabella had returned to her duties. Her demeanor had shifted dramatically; she was colder, more irritable, and distant from her colleagues. Most attributed her behavior to the loss of her twin sister, but whispers about her harshness grew louder. Bella's guardian angel watched silently, deeply concerned about her charge's growing descent into moral darkness.

Jennifer met with her doctor friend. As they discussed Stephanie's case, the doctor revealed his findings. "There's evidence that the decision to operate on Stephanie was premature," he explained. "I believe someone manipulated the records to make it seem necessary. We need to look into this further." Jennifer's heart sank. The threads of deception were tightening, and she vowed to uncover the truth, no matter where it led.

Later that day, Emilia's guardian angel "Mila" spoke in the presence of Jennifer. Her gentle, luminous form exuded calm as she addressed Emilia. "Your courage in admitting the truth to Adam, despite the pain it caused, is commendable. Honesty is a difficult path, but it is also the most fruitful. You have taken the first step toward redemption, and I encourage you to continue on this path. In time, your sincerity and integrity will guide you and those around you toward healing and resolution." Emilia, though still weighed down by guilt, felt a flicker of hope at his words, her resolve to uncover the truth and make amends strengthening.

Emilia sat back on her couch and wondered what will happen to Sam. What will Adam do? Can he forgive him or will he report him to the police? So many unanswered questions.

Two days had passed since the heated confrontation at Adam's home. The house, once filled with the innocent laughter of a baby and the budding warmth of a new love, now echoed with a heavy silence. Adam sat alone in the living room, the soft flicker of the fireplace casting long shadows on the walls. His thoughts swirled, a chaotic mixture of guilt, anger, and longing. The absence of Jennifer weighed heavily on him, as did the words she had spoken before leaving. He missed her deeply, her gentle presence, and her unwavering support.

On the other side of town, Jennifer sat in her modest apartment, staring blankly at her phone. The memory of Adam's outburst still stung, but it couldn't overshadow the longing she felt to be by his side. She wanted to help him heal, to make him understand her true intentions. As if drawn by an invisible force, her phone buzzed. It was Adam.

His voice, low and hesitant, came through the line. "Jennifer, can you come over? I... I think we need to talk."

Jennifer's heart raced as she replied, "I'll be there soon." Without hesitation, she grabbed her coat and rushed out the door.

When Jennifer arrived at Adam's house, the door opened before she could knock. Adam stood there, his eyes reflecting the weight of his emotions. Without a word, Jennifer stepped inside, and as soon as she saw him, she fell into his arms. He held her tightly, as though afraid to let go.

Now calmer, Adam led her to the living room. They sat on the couch, the fire casting a warm glow as Jennifer began to speak. Her voice was steady but laced with emotion.

"Adam," she began, "I need you to understand everything. Emilia and Sam—their story—it's complicated. Emilia and Sam

118

were deeply in love. They planned a life together, but everything shattered after the accident. Sam couldn't admit his guilt. He was paralyzed by fear and shame, and Emilia tried everything to convince him to come forward. When he refused, it broke her. She ended their relationship, even though it tore her apart."

Jennifer's eyes filled with tears as she continued. "Emilia's involvement in your life began out of guilt, but it became so much more. She truly cares for you, Adam. She respects you. She has stood by you, not to cover for Sam, but to be a real friend. I've seen how much she values your friendship. She told me many times that her biggest regret was not telling you sooner, but finding the right moment felt impossible."

Adam listened intently; his gaze fixed on Jennifer as she spoke. He could see the sincerity in her eyes.

"And then there's me," Jennifer said, her voice faltering. "Adam, I did know the truth but was terrified and was not my duty to tell you. I stayed silent because I believed Emilia when she said she'd tell you when the time was right. But my silence doesn't mean I didn't care. I fell in love with you, with your daughter. My feelings for you are real, and they've always been sincere."

Jennifer's voice broke as she pleaded, "Please, Adam, do what you feel is right. If you need to report this to the police, Emilia will understand. She told me she would support your decision no matter what. All she ever wanted was for you to find peace."

Adam's expression softened as he absorbed her words. He reached for Jennifer's hand, his voice steady but filled with emotion. "Jennifer, I'm in love with you. I don't know what to do next, but I need time to think, to decide how to move forward."

Jennifer nodded, respecting his need for space. She stood, retrieved a bottle of red wine, and opened it. Together, they sat on the floor by the glowing fire, the warmth providing a comforting backdrop as they spoke softly. The tension between them dissolved as their conversation grew more intimate. Laughter mixed with tears, and before long, their shared vulnerability drew them closer. They embraced, their kisses leading to a deeper connection as the night unfolded.

When morning arrived, Jennifer woke first. She lay in bed, holding Adam's hand, her thoughts drifting to the conversation she had with her doctor friend. Something about Stephanie's medical records didn't add up. She turned to Adam, her voice gentle. "There's something I need to tell you. It might be nothing, but my doctor friend noticed inconsistencies in Stephanie's hospital records. I'm going to look into it further."

Adam nodded, appreciating her honesty. After Jennifer left, Adam sat in the quiet of his home, deep in thought. He called out to his guardian angel, who appeared in a flash of radiant light.

"What should I do?" Adam asked, his voice heavy with uncertainty.

The guardian angel's voice was calm yet firm. "Adam, you have two choices. You can confront Sam and offer forgiveness, or you can report him to the police to face justice. Both paths will bring closure, but only you can decide which aligns with your heart."

Adam frowned; his brow furrowed. "Forgiveness? After what he's done?"

The angel's gaze softened. "Forgiveness is the utmost form of courage, Adam. But before you act, ensure that Stephanie's death is truly his responsibility. Some things may not be as they seem. Think carefully."

The angel's words lingered as he vanished, leaving Adam deep in thought.

Chapter 15 – Truths in the Shadows

Meanwhile, Emilia met with Sam. She told him everything—her confession to Adam, his reaction, and his need for time. Sam's face paled as he listened, but a newfound resolve began to take shape within him.

"It's time," Sam said finally. "I need to face Adam, to accept the consequences of what I've done."

Emilia's eyes filled with pride. For the first time in months, she saw the man she fell in love with. Her guardian angel appeared beside her, her voice steady. "Sam, you're making the right choice. Sometimes we fall to learn how to rise again." Emilia shared with Sam her guardian comment, and Sam inquired if she is still seeing the angels, which she confirmed and replied, "She will be here till we close this matter and move on."

At the hospital, Dr. Isabella sat in her office, her guardian angel by her side. The weight of her actions pressed heavily on her.

She spoke aloud; her voice filled with despair. "I've lost my way. I killed someone to save my sister, and it was all for nothing. What's left for me now?"

The angel's voice was calm but firm. "Dr. Bella, the choices you made were wrong, but the path forward is yours to decide. Will you seek redemption, or will you continue down this path?"

Bella's eyes hardened. "I am who I am. A killer. Turning myself in won't bring anyone back. Leave me be."

The angel's gaze never wavered. "The consequences of your actions are inevitable. How severe they are depending on what you do next."

Bella stood abruptly. "This meeting is over. Let me live with my choices." As the angel vanished, Dr. Bella stared out the window, her reflection fragmented against the glass, her soul torn between remorse and defiance.

Jennifer's investigation into Stephanie's hospital records took a dramatic and consuming turn. For days, she poured over the documents her doctor friend had shared, each new discrepancy pulling her deeper into the realization that something was profoundly wrong. The timelines didn't add up—Stephanie's surgery had been approved under the pretext of urgency, yet her earlier scans suggested a stable condition that didn't require immediate intervention. The implications of this manipulation sent chills down Jennifer's spine.

Late one night, Jennifer sat at her kitchen table, the dim light overhead casting harsh shadows on the papers sprawled before her. Her doctor friend, Dr. Matthews, sat across from her, his face etched with concern. "You're sure you want to pursue this?" he asked, leaning forward. "This isn't just about uncovering the truth anymore. There could be consequences."

Jennifer's resolve hardened. "I don't care about the consequences," she said firmly. "Stephanie deserves justice. If there's even a chance that Dr. Bella manipulated these records, it's my responsibility to find out why."

Across town, Adam's own emotional turmoil mirrored Jennifer's. The revelation that Sam had been involved in Stephanie's death had left him reeling. He hadn't yet processed his feelings, but he knew one thing: he needed answers. Late in the evening, his phone buzzed with a message from Sam, asking to meet. Adam hesitated, his thumb hovering over the screen. After a long moment, he replied, agreeing to the meeting.

The next day, the two men sat across from each other in a quiet park. The tension between them was palpable. Sam's face was pale, his hands trembling as he clasped them together. Adam's jaw was set, his gaze unyielding.

"I... I don't know where to start," Sam stammered, breaking the silence.

Adam's voice was low and measured. "The beginning is usually a good place."

Sam took a shaky breath. "It was an accident," he began. "I didn't see the van until it was too late. I panicked and drove away. Every day since, I've been haunted by what I did."

Adam's fists clenched. "And you thought running away was the answer? That hiding the truth would somehow erase what you did?"

Sam's voice cracked. "I was a coward, Adam. I was afraid. Of losing Emilia, of facing the consequences. But I see now that I can't live like this anymore. I... I need to make it right."

Adam's anger simmered just beneath the surface, but his guardian angel's words echoed in his mind. Some things may not be as they seem. He took a deep breath, forcing himself to remain composed. "Making it right doesn't erase what you did. It doesn't bring Stephanie back."

"I know," Sam whispered. "But I'm willing to face whatever comes. I just need you to know how sorry I am."

The meeting ended without resolution, leaving Adam to wrestle with his conflicted emotions. He walked away from Sam, his thoughts a whirlwind of anger, pain, and uncertainty.

Back at the hospital, Jennifer's investigation had reached a critical point. She scheduled a meeting with Dr. Bella, determined to confront her directly. Bella's office was austere, the air thick with tension as Jennifer stepped inside. Bella greeted her with a thin smile that didn't reach her eyes.

"To what do I owe the pleasure?" Dr. Bella asked coldly, gesturing for Jennifer to sit.

Jennifer wasted no time. "There are discrepancies in Stephanie's medical records," she said bluntly. "Timelines and decisions that don't add up." I'm here to give you a chance to explain before I take this to the hospital board."

Bella's expression hardened. "Are you accusing me of something?" she asked, her voice icy.

Jennifer held her gaze. "I'm asking for the truth."

Bella leaned back in her chair, her eyes narrowing. "Be careful, Jennifer. Accusations like these can have serious consequences."

Jennifer stood, her resolve unshaken. "So can falsifying medical records. I'll give you until the end of the week to come clean. After that, I'm taking this to the board."

Bella watched her leave, her hands gripping the armrests of her chair. Her guardian angel appeared beside her, a quiet presence amidst the storm of her thoughts.

"You know what you did was wrong," the angel said softly. "It's not too late to make amends."

Bella's jaw tightened. "Leave me alone," she muttered. "I've already lost everything. What good will confessing do now?"

The angel sighed, its form flickering slightly. "The path to redemption is never easy, but it's always worth taking."

Bella's gaze hardened as the angel faded away. She turned her attention to the papers on her desk, determined to maintain her facade, no matter the cost.

Jennifer's week was filled with tense meetings and sleepless nights. Her conversations with Adam became a source of solace, their shared pain forging a deeper connection. She updated him on her findings, and together they began to piece together the full picture of Stephanie's final days.

She raced across town to meet Dr. Matthews, her pulse quickening as her mind spun with possibilities. The inconsistencies she'd already uncovered had painted a troubling picture, but her gut told her there was more. At the hospital, Matthews greeted her with a grave expression and a folder tucked under his arm.

"You were right," he said without preamble, leading her into an empty conference room. He spread the documents across the table. "This signature for urgent surgery does not have a supporting report."

Jennifer's breath caught. "Signed? By who?"

Matthews hesitated, his fingers brushing over a name on the form. "It points to Dr. Bella. She signed off on the surgery as urgent, but the earlier reports contradict that urgency. It's clear manipulation." He continued to express his concerns, adding another layer of doubt. He discovered that Stephanie's heart was donated to Dr. Isabella's twin sister, and the transplant operation was performed the same day as her death.

Jennifer's hands trembled as she heard the news. This was the smoking gun she'd been searching for, but it brought her no relief. Instead, a wave of dread washed over her. Dr. Bella's actions weren't just unethical; they were criminal, she thought.

She slumped into a chair, her mind reeling. "These changes everything," she murmured. "I need to talk to Adam."

Later that evening, Jennifer met Adam at his home. The fire crackled in the hearth as she laid the documents before him. He scanned them in silence, his face a mask of controlled emotion. When he finally looked up, his eyes were filled with anger and hurt.

"So, Dr. Isabella... She manipulated everything? She's responsible for pushing the surgery before it was necessary?"

Jennifer nodded; her voice was soft. "It looks that way."

Adam leaned back, running a hand through his hair. "This doesn't just hurt... it complicates everything. If Bella's actions led to Stephanie's death, then Sam... he might not be the only one at fault."

Jennifer reached for his hand, her touch grounding him. "We'll figure it out, Adam. Together."

Meanwhile, Bella's erratic behavior escalated. At the hospital, she lashed out at a junior colleague who questioned her decisions. The incident drew attention, whispers spreading among the staff. Her guardian angel watched from the corner of her office, silent but present.

"You can still turn back," the angel said softly, though Bella ignored it. Her defiance grew, each decision pushing her further away from redemption.

Jennifer and Dr. Matthews began compiling a case to present to the hospital board. The weight of the truth pressed heavily on them both, but they knew it was necessary. The pieces were falling into place, and the shadows surrounding Stephanie's death were finally beginning to lift.

Chapter 16: Twists and Turns

Adam sat across from Jennifer in a dimly lit coffee shop. The air around them seemed heavy with unspoken truths. Jennifer leaned forward; her voice was low but urgent. "Adam, we both know something doesn't add up about Stephanie's death. If there was manipulation of the hospital records, we have to uncover it."

Adam nodded; his jaw clenched. "I can't stop thinking about it. There's a shadow over all of this—Dr. Isabella's twin sister's heart transplant, Stephanie's death, and hospital records that don't look right. It's too coincidental."

Jennifer's determination was palpable. "We need to investigate further. It's clear this isn't just a tragic accident. There was a motive."

That night, as Adam sat alone in his apartment, his guardian angel appeared, radiating calm. Adam looked up; exhaustion etched on his face.

"Adam," the angel began, "your instincts are right. There is a truth buried here, one that demands justice. It's time to act."

Adam leaned back, running a hand through his hair. "But how? Where do I even start?"

The angel's voice was firm yet soothing. "Go to the hospital director. Share your suspicions. Request a formal investigation. You cannot shoulder this alone." Emboldened by his angel's words, Adam resolved to meet with the director the following day.

In the director's office, Adam's hands trembled as he recounted his concerns about Dr. Isabella and the inconsistencies in Stephanie's records. The director, a serious man with sharp features, listened intently. His expression grew grave as Adam finished.

"These are serious allegations," the director said, his tone measured. "If what you're saying is true, it's a breach of medical ethics on an unprecedented level. I will initiate a formal investigation immediately." True to his word, the director convened the hospital's board, sharing Adam's suspicions and pledging to uncover the truth.

Meanwhile, Adam wrestled with another decision: reporting Sam to the police for the hit-and-run. He confided in Jennifer, who had become his closest confidante.

"I can't live with this guilt," Adam admitted. "Sam's actions that night led to Stephanie's death. He has to be held accountable."

Jennifer placed a hand on his arm. "I understand, but please wait until the hospital's investigation is complete. If we're right about Dr. Isabella, her actions changed everything. Let's uncover the full story first." Reluctantly, Adam agreed to delay his report.

Jennifer visited Emilia and Sam for dinner, her presence casting a somber shadow over the evening. She detailed the findings so far, including the potential falsification of records and Dr. Isabella's connection to the transplant.

Sam leaned back, relief flickering across his face. "So, Stephanie's death wasn't entirely my fault."

Jennifer's tone sharpened. "That doesn't absolve you, Sam. Adam plans to report you to the police. He's determined to see justice served." Sam's face paled, but he nodded. "If that's what it takes, I'll face the consequences."

Later that night, Angel Mila, her face grave. "Emilia, there is more to this than you realize. The trouble angels manipulated Dr. Isabella, preying on her desperation to save her sister. Their influence led to the falsification of records and ultimately, Stephanie's death."

Emilia was stunned. "Trouble angels? They were behind this?"

The angel nodded. "Their interference disrupted the natural order, forcing Dr. Isabella to choose a path of deceit."

Desperate for clarity, Emilia called Jennifer. "Bella manipulated the records. It's true. We have to expose her."

Determined to find the truth, Emilia hired Michael, a formidable lawyer known for his unyielding pursuit of justice. Michael, armed with a formal authorization from Adam, approached the hospital demanding access to all relevant records. The board, eager to avoid legal repercussions, cooperated fully, delivering stacks of documents to Michael's team.

The hospital director summoned Dr. Isabella to discuss the growing doubts surrounding her actions. Bella, pale and defensive, denied any wrongdoing.

"I based my decisions on the lab analysis," she insisted, though her voice faltered.

The director's eyes narrowed. "The heart transplant to your twin sister raises questions that cannot be ignored. We will uncover the truth." Suspended pending the investigation, Bella left the hospital in a panic.

At home, Bella sought solace in her guardian angel, who urged her to confess. But her fear of imprisonment overpowered her conscience. She attempted to summon her trouble angel, closing her eyes and imagining his mocking grin.

"What now?" she thought. "If they find that I falsified the report, I'll lose everything. Maybe I should disappear, go back to Mexico."

The board's inquiry uncovered that the report issued to proceed with the operation does not match Stephanie's lab and scan results, raising doubts. The responsible doctor at the lab, a seasoned professional, denied authoring the falsified report.

"Stephanie and her baby had strong chances of survival," he asserted. "Someone replaced the original findings in the system."

Jennifer's relentless investigation finally uncovered irrefutable evidence that Dr. Isabella had falsified medical records. The hospital's IT manager, working closely with the director, unearthed a digital trail: Bella had uploaded the falsified scans herself, altering Sarah's records to prioritize her twin sister's heart transplant. The revelation was damning. Confronted by the hospital board, Bella maintained her composure, vehemently denying all wrongdoing.

"This is preposterous," she said, her voice steady despite the cold sweat trickling down her spine. "There must be some mistake in the system."

However, the evidence overshadowed her denials. Each piece of data pointed squarely at her. As the board members debated the next steps, Bella's carefully constructed facade began to crack. Panic clawed at her insides as she realized her career—and possibly her freedom—was slipping away.

Meanwhile, Adam arrived at the hospital with his newborn daughter, Lily, for a routine follow-up checkup. Unaware of the storm brewing around Dr. Isabella, he waited in the nursery while the nurse prepared Lily's records. Dr. Bella, passing by in a panic mode, spotted them. The sight of Adam's innocent child triggered a desperate, unthinkable plan in her unraveling mind.

Moments later, chaos erupted. Lily was missing. The hospital staff scoured the nursery and surrounding halls in vain. Surveillance footage quickly provided the shocking answer: Dr. Isabella had taken the baby.

Adam was inconsolable. His cries of anguish echoed through the hospital halls as Jennifer, Emilia, and Sam rushed to his side. The moment they arrived, Adam's grief boiled over into anger. He turned on Sam, his eyes blazing with fury.

"This is your fault," Adam snarled. "You destroyed my life".

Sam recoiled, guilt and shame flickering across his face.

"Adam, enough!" Jennifer interjected firmly, placing herself between the two men. "This isn't helping. Right now, we need to focus on finding Lily. Every second counts."

Emilia nodded, her voice steady despite the tension. "She's right. We're wasting time fighting. Dr. Bella's out there with Lily. We need to act."

Emilia pored over surveillance footage alongside the team. Her sharp eyes caught Bella's car leaving the hospital along with the baby inside. She obtained the car color and tag plate from the hospital records to report it to the police.

"There," Emilia pointed, her voice urgent. "She headed that way 10 minutes ago. We can still catch her if we move fast."

Adam, galvanized by this lead, didn't hesitate. "Let's go," he said, his voice firm with determination.

Jennifer, Emilia, Sam, and Adam gathered outside the hospital, their guardian angels hovering close. Despite their differences and lingering tensions, they united under a shared purpose: to find Lily and bring her home.

Chapter 17: The Pursuit of Truth

The urgency of the situation dictated swift action, and the team made the critical decision to split up. Each route they chose bristled with potential dangers and the looming threat of failure. They felt the silent vigilance of their guardian angels, whose ethereal presence offered a semblance of comfort amidst the turmoil.

Adam, with his jaw set and his hands clenched around the steering wheel, pushed his car to its limits along the highway. The night swallowed Dr. Isabella's car, leaving him chasing shadows and the faint hope that he was still on the right track. He glanced periodically at his guardian angel, whose serene demeanor belied the gravity of their pursuit.

"Adam, trust in your resolve," the angel's voice resonated, clear despite the roar of the engine and the rush of the wind. "The echoes of Stephanie's plea for justice fuel your pursuit. Let that strength guide you."

Adam responded to the empty seat beside him, his voice thick with emotion. "Stephanie, I won't let this be in vain. I swear I'll make things right." His words hung in the charged air of the car, a solemn vow to the silent night.

The highway stretched before him like a dark river, its currents strong and unforgiving. Time seemed to dilate, each minute stretching out before snapping back with the jolt of his heartbeats, reminding him of what was at stake.

Meanwhile, Jennifer navigated the bureaucratic maze of the local police station with a calm demeanor that masked her internal frenzy. "I need to report a kidnapping linked to a severe case of medical malpractice," she asserted to the desk officer, her voice a beacon of urgency in the quiet hum of the station.

The officer, initially skeptical, sharpened his focus as Jennifer unfolded the details of Dr. Isabella's desperate actions and the dire implications of her meddling with medical records. Nodding gravely, he assured her, "We'll issue a search warrant immediately and dispatch units to track down the suspect's vehicle."

Jennifer stepped back into the chilly night, her breath visible in the air as she updated Adam with a quick phone call, her words a mixture of hope and anxiety.

Simultaneously, Emilia and Sam approached Dr. Isabella's apartment with a mix of haste and dread. The building loomed ominously, its lights dim, the shadows deep. They were met with the guarded words of a neighbor who confirmed Bella's brief and frantic appearance to grab some belongings. "She was in a rush, looked scared," the neighbor whispered, peering from behind a barely opened door.

Emilia's face set in determination as she turned to Sam. "She's on the run, but she won't get far. We need to predict her next move." Consulting her phone, she quickly arranged for a private investigator to track Bella's movements, their conversation a rapid exchange of information and strategy.

Dr. Bella, meanwhile, drove through the winding back roads with a wild look in her eyes, her mind racing as fast as her car. The isolation of the rural route reflected her internal state—cut off, desperate, veering towards the unpredictable. Her guardian angel's voice was a soft whisper lost in the cacophony of her thoughts.

"There is still time to choose a different path, one of honesty and redemption," the angel implored softly.

But Bella's mind was a fortress now, sealed against remorse or reason. She arrived at a secluded cottage hidden deep in the woods, the structure barely more than a shadow under the moon's dim glow. Inside, her plans grew darker as she considered her few remaining options, each more desperate than the last.

The private investigator, following the slimmest of clues, scoured Bella's apartment. The breakthrough came when he found a photo of Bella standing before a quaint, obscurely located cottage. The image, a stark contrast to her current fugitive status, offered a vital clue.

Back at Adam's house, the team reconvened, weariness etched on their faces but spirits bolstered by a collective resolve. They shared their findings and strategized late into the night. "She can't have gone far," Adam murmured, the image of his daughter driving him beyond the brink of exhaustion.

Jennifer, touching his shoulder gently, reassured him. "We're close, Adam. We'll bring her back." Her confidence was a lifeline in the swirling uncertainty.

As the group prepared to disperse for a few brief hours of rest, Adam found himself momentarily alone, leaning heavily against the cool surface of his car. The weight of the night's events pressed down on him with an unbearable force. In the silence of the early morning, the reality of his daughter's absence tore through the last vestiges of his composure. His daughter, his little Lily, was out there somewhere, her safety hanging by a thread, and the helplessness he felt was suffocating.

Adam slid down to the ground, his back against the car, and buried his face in his hands. His body shook with silent sobs, each breath a struggle against the despair threatening to engulf him. "Lily," he whispered into the void, his voice cracking, "I'm so sorry. Daddy's here, and I'm coming for you. Just hang on." The thought of her innocent eyes, usually so full of laughter and life, now possibly clouded with confusion and fear, pierced his heart like a cold blade. He wiped the tears from his cheeks, steeling himself with the image of her joyful smile, using it as a shield against the darkness of his thoughts. The night air felt heavy with his whispered promises, each word a vow to restore the light to his daughter's world. With a deep, steadying breath,

Adam pushed himself up, the resolve hardening in his eyes. He couldn't afford to break—not now, not when Lily needed him most.

With the dawn barely breaking, the local police expanded their search, circulating details of Dr. Bella's vehicle to every available unit. The private investigator's discovery of the cottage's potential location reinvigorated the search, turning it into a focused hunt that spanned county lines.

As the sun rose, casting long shadows and bringing the promise of a new day, Adam, Jennifer, Emilia, and Sam faced the horizon with a hardened determination. The race against time had taken on a new urgency, but they were united, stronger together, with the silent support of their celestial watchers. They prepared for what could be the final confrontation, knowing that the hours ahead would test their resolve like never before.

Chapter 18: Breaking Dawn

As the first tendrils of morning light crept over the horizon, the shadows of the night began to retreat, chased away by the promise of a new day. It was in these early, delicate moments that a meeting of celestial guides took place, orchestrated under the discreet vigilance of the Chief of Angels. Dr. Bella's guardian angel, a being radiant with compassionate light, sought out Emilia's guardian angel in an urgent conference. There, amid the ethereal glow of dawn, the location of the secluded cottage was revealed—a critical piece of intelligence that could change the course of events.

Emilia's guardian angel, a figure of serene authority, wasted no time in conveying this vital information. With a whisper that seemed to echo through the spiritual ether, the coordinates of Bella's hideout were passed down to Emilia, who received the message with a sharp intake of breath.

"We've found her," Emilia announced, her voice slicing through the early morning stillness with urgency. In the makeshift headquarters, a room illuminated by the soft glow of multiple screens and a single overhead light, Adam, Jennifer, and Sam converged around the map spread out on the central table. Their faces were etched with exhaustion and determination, the map a tableau of possibilities and peril.

Adam's fingers trembled as they hovered over the marked location, a remote area outlined with a red circle. "That's it," he whispered hoarsely, "That's where she's hiding."

Jennifer, ever the orchestrator, took immediate action, her phone pressed tightly against her ear as she communicated with the private investigator who had been on standby throughout the night. "We have a location. Meet us halfway, and bring everything you've got. We need to handle this delicately and securely."

The group moved with a swift, driven energy, fueled by the determination to bring the ordeal to a close. The drive to the cottage was laden with tension. Each mile they covered brought them closer to a confrontation they had been preparing for, yet nothing could truly prepare them for what awaited.

Adam's mind was a whirlwind of fear and hope, his daughter's image—her smile, her laughter, her innocence—flashing before his eyes like a beacon guiding him forward. He gripped the steering wheel tighter, his knuckles white, as he navigated the dark, winding roads that led to the cottage.

Upon arriving at the edge of the dense woods where the private investigator's car was already parked, the group gathered for a quick briefing. The investigator, a seasoned professional with years of experience in delicate situations, was ready with a plan.

"We approach with caution," he instructed firmly, checking his equipment one last time. "Our priority is the safety of the child and the peaceful apprehension of Dr. Isabella. No heroics—we do this by the book."

With nods of agreement, the team advanced into the woods, their movements silent and coordinated, the crunch of leaves under their feet muffled by the thick moss that carpeted the forest floor. The cottage soon came into view, a dark, foreboding structure that seemed to absorb the weak light of dawn rather than reflect it.

Peering through a cracked window, they could see Dr. Bella pacing the dimly lit interior, her figure tense and agitated as she clutched the baby to her chest. The sight of his daughter so close yet so far sent a surge of mixed emotions through Adam, fueling his resolve.

The private investigator signaled them to hold position as he approached the door. With a practiced ease, he quietly opened it and stepped inside, his presence commanding yet non-threatening.

Dr. Bella froze, her eyes wide with shock and fear. "It's over, Dr. Isabella," he announced calmly. "We're here to make sure everyone is safe, especially the baby."

"You don't understand," Bella cried out, desperation cracking her voice as she held the baby tighter to her chest. "I had to do it. I had no choice!"

At that moment, her guardian angel stepped forward, invisible to all but Bella, and whispered soothing words that cut through her panic. "Isabella, let go of your burden. Trust that there is a path to redemption through honesty and repentance."

With a profound internal struggle visible on her face, Bella slowly loosened her grip on the baby, tears streaming down her cheeks as the realization of her actions and their consequences finally seemed to dawn on her.

The investigator quickly and gently took the baby into his arms, ensuring her safety before turning his attention back to Bella. "Come with us, Dr. Isabella. Let's sort this out the right way."

Adam rushed forward, his arms outstretched as he took his daughter from the investigator. Holding her close, he felt a flood of relief so intense it nearly brought him to his knees. "Thank you," he choked out, his voice thick with emotion as he looked over at Emilia and the others. "I couldn't have done this without all of you."

As the police arrived to secure the scene, the morning light began to strengthen, casting long shadows and illuminating the faces of those who had endured through the night. Dr. Isabella was taken into custody, her fate a tapestry of legal battles and moral reckonings that would unfold in the days to come.

The return journey was quiet, each member of the team lost in their own thoughts, the weight of the night's events settling around them like a heavy cloak. But within Adam's heart, there was a lightness—a relief so profound it almost felt like a rebirth.

The subsequent celebration at Sam's house was a muted affair, the joy of the baby's safe return tempered by the gravity of what had transpired. They toasted to truth, to justice, and to the unbreakable bond that had formed among them under the most harrowing of circumstances.

But the journey was far from over. The courtroom awaited, a stern arena where the full measure of justice would be sought for Stephanie's tragic demise. The trial unfolded over several days, a meticulous dissection of Dr. Bella's actions and decisions. Witnesses took the stand one by one, their testimonies weaving a compelling narrative of manipulation and desperation that had led to irrevocable consequences.

Dr. Bella's defense attorney worked tirelessly, attempting to shift the narrative, to paint a picture of a woman driven by familial love rather than cold calculation. They called Sam to the stand, hoping his admission of the hit-and-run would somehow mitigate Bella's actions.

Sam's testimony was heartfelt and raw. "I made an unforgivable mistake," he admitted, his voice laden with regret. "But my actions, while reckless, did not lead directly to Stephanie's death. That was a result of decisions made by Dr. Isabella under circumstances I had no part in."

When it was Adam's turn to testify, the courtroom hung on his every word. He recounted the harrowing events, Bella's escalating desperation, and her ultimate decision to kidnap his daughter. But as his testimony neared its end, Adam did something unexpected. He stood, his posture straight, his voice clear and resonant.

"Your Honor," he began, addressing the judge with a solemnity that commanded attention. "While we seek justice today for what has been done to my family, to Stephanie, I must speak a truth that weighs heavily on my heart."

The courtroom was silent, the air thick with anticipation.

"The night of the accident, the night that set all these events in motion, I too made a mistake. I was there, at that intersection. I crossed at a red light. If there is blame to be assigned, it must be shared among all parties involved, myself included."

A collective gasp rippled through the spectators, and even the judge seemed momentarily taken aback by Adam's declaration.

It was an act of honesty, of immense moral courage that shifted the atmosphere of the courtroom. Emilia was shocked but she immediately knew that Adam has done this because he decided to forgive Sam. She had a big smile on her face and looked at Sam and gave him a big hug. She looked at Adam and whispered "Thank You".

The trial reached its zenith as Dr. Isabella Bella stood before the court; the weight of her fate palpable in the heavy air of the courtroom. After days of testimony, as her attorney concluded the defense, Dr. Bella requested permission to speak. Granted the floor, she rose, her figure composed yet bearing the scars of deep internal conflict. Her voice, when she spoke, resonated with a mixture of contrition and newfound clarity.

"Your Honor, esteemed members of the court," Dr. Bella began, her voice steady but tinged with emotion, "I stand before you today, a woman who has strayed far from her oath, driven by a desperate love for my sister and a misguided belief that the end could justify the means. I admit to my guilt and deeply regret the pain I have caused."

She paused, gathering her thoughts, her gaze sweeping over the courtroom, lingering on the faces of Adam and others affected by her actions. "Throughout this ordeal, I have grappled with the nature of my actions, the battle between good and evil within me, intensified by what I now understand as the whispers of my trouble angel. This experience has forced me to confront the darkest parts of myself, to see how I allowed fear and desperation to cloud my judgment."

Dr. Bella's voice grew firmer as she delved deeper into her reflection. "I have come to recognize that each of us is accompanied by forces unseen—angels, if you will, that embody our best and worst selves. My trouble angel showed me my darkest desires, pushing me towards decisions that I will regret for the rest of my life. But I also stand here, inspired by the possibility of redemption, guided by what I have learned from my guardian angel, who urged me to embrace truth and seek forgiveness."

She looked down briefly, then back up, her eyes clear. "I used to wonder whether we are truly free, whether our paths are ours to choose or if they are laid out by these spiritual entities. This trial, this error, has taught me that while we may be influenced, the final decisions are ours alone. I chose wrongly, swayed by a darker side I wish I had recognized and combated sooner."

Drawing a deep breath, she concluded, "I am profoundly sorry for the suffering I have caused. To the families impacted, to this court, and to the medical community I once served—I am sorry. I am prepared to accept the consequences of my actions, and it is my sincerest hope that my story serves as a cautionary tale about the perils of losing sight of one's ethical compass in the pursuit of misguided goals."

As she took her seat, the courtroom was enveloped in a heavy silence, her words resonating with a profound intensity. The judge, after a thoughtful pause, acknowledged her candor and the depth of her introspection before delivering the sentence. Dr. Bella was convicted, her punishment severe yet tempered by her acceptance of responsibility and her expressed desire for redemption. Her sentence was to serve as both retribution for her actions and a chance for rehabilitation, reflecting the complex, painfully human elements of her downfall and her search for moral redemption in the aftermath of her tragic missteps.

In the aftermath, as they gathered once again at Sam's house for a quiet dinner, their guardian angels made a rare appearance. "Truth and honesty always prevail," Angel Mila declared, her voice imbued with a gentle authority. "You have all faced incredible challenges, but you chose to confront them with integrity. Remember, we are here to guide, but the decisions are always yours to make."

The evening ended not with a somber tone but with a celebration of the resilience of the human spirit. Laughter filled the room, and stories were shared, each anecdote a testament to their journey through darkness and back into the light.

As the night drew to a close, the angels faded back into the ether, their mission complete. The group, strengthened by their ordeal, looked forward to a future that, while uncertain, was theirs to shape with the same courage and honesty that had seen them through their darkest hours.

Chapter 19 – The Final Dream

The clock struck 4:00 a.m., and Emilia awoke with a start. The familiar, methodical ticking echoed through the stillness of her room, marking an hour that resonated with significance. It was the same hour when her journey had begun weeks ago. As she sat up, her breathing uneven, moonlight streamed through the curtains, casting ghostly shadows that danced on the walls. But tonight, something felt distinctly different.

She scanned the room, her heart racing. The comforting glow of her guardian angel and the impish presence of her trouble angel, both constants during her tumultuous journey, were absent. "Hello?" she called softly into the stillness, her voice trembling slightly. Silence was her only reply; the room remained calm, devoid of the ethereal energy she had grown so accustomed to.

Panic fluttered in her chest as she swung her legs over the bed. Her feet met the cool floor, sending a shiver up her spine. Emilia walked to the corner of the room where her guardian angel had often appeared, dispensing quiet wisdom and gentle reassurances. She reached out, half-expecting to feel a hint of the familiar warm energy, but her fingers grasped only air.

Turning, she glanced toward the foot of her bed where her trouble angel used to sit, his snide remarks slicing through tension, often making her laugh despite the circumstances. The space was empty, the atmosphere uncharged.

"They're gone," she whispered to herself, the reality settling heavily around her. Initially, feelings of abandonment washed over her. They had guided, challenged, and helped her uncover truths she had never dared to face. Now, they had vanished.

But as she stood in the quiet of her bedroom, another realization dawned on her. Perhaps their disappearance was not abandonment but a sign of closure. The events of the past weeks flashed through her mind—the emotional reunion of Adam and his daughter, the revelations in the courtroom, the final, poignant speeches of the angels at the dinner table. Everything had been resolved. Justice had been served. The truth had been laid bare, and through it all, she had grown stronger.

Emilia walked to the window and gazed out at the serene world beyond. The trees swayed gently in the breeze, and a faint glow from a distant streetlamp lit the edges of her garden. Resting her hands on the windowsill, she exhaled deeply. "I guess this is how it's supposed to be," she murmured. "They're gone because they've done their job. My path is clear."

For the first time in what felt like forever, Emilia felt a profound sense of peace. The weight of uncertainty that had shadowed her was gone. She thought of Sam, probably still asleep in the next room, their bond now stronger than ever. She thought of Jennifer, whose humor had brought light to the darkest moments. She thought of Adam, who had found the strength to forgive and move forward. Her angels' absence no longer felt like a loss; it felt like freedom. She had everything she needed to continue on her path—to move forward with strength and clarity. She was no longer the person she had been when this all began. She had faced her fears, confronted her guilt, and emerged more whole than ever before.

Returning to her bed, Emilia pulled the covers over herself, a faint smile touching her lips. She closed her eyes, her mind finally quiet. Sleep claimed her quickly, and she dreamed not of angels or trials but of a future filled with light and love. The echoes of her journey lingered in her heart, not as a burden but as a reminder of how far she had come. And as the night deepened, the clock ticked on, its steady rhythm carrying her into a new dawn.

When Emilia woke again a few hours later, the morning was bright and the memories of her experiences still vivid. She brewed her morning coffee, the rich aroma filling her kitchen, grounding her in the comfort of routine. Her favorite playlist played softly as she drove to the bank, the familiar tunes a soothing backdrop to her thoughts.

Upon entering the bank, she spotted Jennifer at her desk, deep in paperwork. Emilia's face lit up with a warm smile as she approached and wrapped her friend in a big hug. "How is Adam? And how is the baby?" she asked, her eyes sparkling with an irrepressible joy.

Jennifer paused, a puzzled expression crossing her face. "Adam who? And what baby, Emilia?"

Emilia blinked, her smile faltering. "Come on, Jenny. Don't play games. You know who I'm talking about."

Jennifer's confusion deepened. "Emilia, I'm not playing. I really don't know what you're talking about."

A chill ran down Emilia's spine as she stared at Jennifer. "You also don't know Dr. Isabella?" she asked slowly.

Jennifer stood abruptly, her chair scraping the floor. "Emilia, what's gotten into you today? Are you okay?"

Emilia took a step back, her mind racing as she pieced together the truth. "Did we visit the woods last week? And have dinner together?" she pressed.

Jennifer shook her head, firm and clear. "No, Emilia. I've been visiting my mom for the past two weeks. I haven't seen you since then."

Understanding dawned on Emilia, and a slow smile spread across her face. She pulled Jennifer into another hug, this time with a laugh. "Thank you, Jenny. Thank you for being you."

Jennifer returned the smile, albeit still puzzled. "Okay, now I'm officially confused. But you're welcome, I guess?"

Emilia stepped back and quickly dialed Sam's number. His voice, warm and familiar, greeted her. "Sam," she said, her voice brimming with excitement, "I need to see you tonight for dinner at my place. And bring Jennifer too. I have a dream to share with both of you."

Sam's laughter echoed softly through the phone. "Sounds intriguing. I'll be there."

Emilia hung up, her heart light, looking forward to the evening. There was so much to tell, and she couldn't wait to share her profound dream with her closest friends, her earthbound guardian angels.